COLLIDE

OFF-LIMITS #2

PIPER LAWSON

PIPER LAWSON BOOKS

Content editing by Becca Mysoor
Line and copy editing by Erica Russikoff
Cover photography by Regina Wamba

Collide (verb):

Come into conflict or opposition.

1
———

OLIVIA

*I*t's easy to look at someone's life and think, *they've got it all together.*

They've never had their heart broken, or gone without, or been told they're not enough.

All I wanted was to be closer to this man who makes me feel things I've never felt before, want things I've never let myself want.

And I got my wish.

Until yesterday.

The train ride back to campus is a blur. Adam and Royce talk about sports and the competition and other things I tune out. Madison sits silent, her face buried in a textbook.

Last night keeps replaying in my mind.

Sawyer's frustration and anger. Madison's shock exiting the elevator.

Putting together whatever she heard, plus my tear-stained face and Sawyer's posture, it took all of two seconds for her to size up the situation and cross the hall.

"You need to leave, Professor Redmond."

I expected him to tell her to stay out of it, but with a last look of agitation, he complied.

"Are you hurt?" she asked me.

"No." Not how she meant. "Thank you," I started, but she stalked past me for the bathroom.

"Don't talk to me and go the fuck to sleep."

Today when the train arrives at Elmwood, I get in a cab without looking back.

Now, every step, my legs feel heavy. Like ballet practice the morning after I went drinking for the first time with some classmates from school.

He didn't care about me—I was a type to him. A challenge for his reckless soul, a way to say fuck you to the world that did him wrong.

I want to curl up in a ball, but I'll settle for a shower and a coffee in private before I have to figure out what to do about Madison.

When I drag myself up the stairs of our building and unlock the door of my apartment, Jules sits on the arm of the couch. Kat leans over the back of a chair. Planted in the center of the couch is my sister.

"Emma. What are you doing here?" I blink. I'm probably seeing things after a hellish twelve hours.

"I had a fight with Trey. My boyfriend," she adds for Kat and Jules' benefit. "We were supposed to go out this weekend and I had it all planned but he bailed. Mom told me she talked to him and that's why." She bursts into tears.

I set my bag down by the door and cross to her, folding her in my arms. "Hey, it's okay."

The couch creaks as I sink onto it, and I stroke her hair like when we were kids.

"Mom said he was a psychopath."

"That's dramatic." Sure, he's older and has a bike, but psychopath might be a stretch.

"Where were you last night?" she mumbles against my shoulder.

"In the city for a school thing."

Kat and Jules exchange a look.

I shift on the couch to get more comfortable, only something lumpy prods at my butt.

"Ahhh!"

I reach under the cushion and spot a purple vibrator the size of a large vegetable. I pinch it gingerly between my fingers before tossing it at Kat.

"Oh, that one's mine," Jules says, reaching for it.

"For future reference, Emma, all problems can be solved by vibrators," Kat says breezily.

"Or not dating guys in the first place." Jules shrugs.

Emma sniffs from the couch, looking between them wide-eyed, then back at me.

"Does Mom know you're here?"

A defiant head toss. "No. Don't try to make me go home," Emma warns. "I won't do it."

I want to be alone. But if I can't be, then I have to get out of here.

Out of this room. Out of this school. Out of this neighborhood.

"I have an idea," I start.

The four of us spend the day exploring town, going to Some Like It Hot for coffee and pastries, taking bikes around campus and hitting Jules' favorite vintage store.

I send a text to Madison in between, as I pause flipping through a rack of summer dresses and shorts.

Liv: I get that you don't want to talk, but we need to.

. . .

There's no answer, but I can't help looking at another chain of texts.

Unknown: Olivia. Please talk to me.

Unknown: Come on.

"Enough phone." Emma swipes it out of my hand before I can stop her.

"Emma, give that back!"

"Why? What's so important?" She looks down at the screen, and my pulse accelerates. She swipes through the text messages. "Oh my God. Who is this guy?"

Shit.

"No one." I manage to get the phone back, but she looks hurt.

"It's not Adam. Adam wouldn't talk like that."

"It's some guy I've been hanging out with." It sounds totally inadequate.

"But now you're fighting."

"Yeah."

He lied to me. About who he is. What we are.

"That reminds me... Are you and Trey hooking up?"

"That's why Mom lost her shit. She found my condoms. But we haven't had a chance." Emma pulls out a hanger without looking at me, holding up the dark purple skirt against her body. "It's not a big deal."

"Sex is always a big deal."

"So you're supposed to be in love? You made Adam follow you around to fundraisers and parties for years before you let him in your pants and look how that turned out."

"That's not what I mean. Even if it's casual, you need to trust the other person."

She slings the skirt over one shoulder. "The new guy. Is he in your class?"

"He's from school." I flip through more clothes on the rack.

"And with this mystery guy, it's different. Better."

"Yes, it's better." At her curious look, I force myself to go on. "With Adam, I felt like I was going through the motions. Performing some routine, and my heart wasn't in it."

Her sigh is half groan. "The fucked-up thing about Mom is I'm being responsible. He doesn't want anything to do with condoms. I'm the one who told him I won't do it without. Because that's some shit

I'm not asking for." She slides a look at me. "You've never..."

"Gone without? No."

It always felt as if Sawyer was touching the deepest parts of me with a look, a kiss, a smile. Him inside me with nothing between us would be devastating.

"Listen, Ems. Don't accept less than you deserve. You want a guy who treats you well. Who's honest with you and wants you for who you are."

"I get that." Her lips curve. "But Trey's also super hot."

***

The karaoke place is a basement dive on the same side of town as Velvet, though not as far out.

"Have you ever done karaoke?" Jules asks Emma as we head down the stairs.

"No."

I raise an eyebrow at the short purple skirt. There seemed to be more fabric when my sister pulled it off the rack at the store.

She catches me. "Like you can talk, Sister Stripper."

I flip her off and she gasps. "Wow, first you ditch the cashmere"—she nods to my dark jeans and black heeled boots—"and now this." She studies me hard. "Where's your necklace?"

"I guess I outgrew it." My hand itches to reach for the pendant that's sat near my collarbone for five years. "You're in the presence of karaoke royalty," I say to change the subject.

Kat grins. "Nice to meet you. I can slay any song."

"I thought you were the one in performing arts?" Emma asks Jules, confused.

"I am. She's the one with the attention crisis."

We find a table in the back of the bar and order beers. The room is dark and packed.

I sneak another look at my phone—nothing new from Sawyer, or from Madison.

It's the weekend, so I doubt she's reporting us today, but next week is fall reading week which means plenty of time to turn us in.

"I'm not sure I want to do this," Emma says, looking around.

"It's karaoke, not a death sentence. You've been thrown twenty feet in the air for cheerleading stunts," I remind her. "It's about believing in yourself and trying new things. So let's have fun."

"Give it a shot," Kat tells Emma.

My sister does.

Taylor Swift's song, "All Too Well," comes over the speakers.

While Emma's up there singing a breakup song that hits a little too close to home, Jules leans over. "What happened this weekend?"

I drum my fingers on the tabletop, not quite hitting the beat. "I learned Sawyer has a type, and apparently I'm it."

Emma hits a high note. It's not close to being on key, but she goes for it.

"Before he left New York, that got him in trouble. It's the reason he walked away from his company."

"And when you asked him about it, he said..." Jules trails off and I reach for my drink.

The beer is cool on my tongue, the sweetness cutting into the hops.

"It's obvious, isn't it? He likes wanting what he shouldn't."

I down the rest of the beer then shift out of my seat and head to the bar for a refill.

We never talked about an exclusive relationship, and whatever went down is in the past. But it bothers the hell out of me because I thought what we had was special.

The bartender fulfills my order and I'm turning back when another figure heading for the exit runs into me.

The three glasses I'm carrying spill, beer

splashing up my arms and onto my clothes before the glasses tumble to the dirty carpet.

"Shit, I'm..." Madison starts, before taking me in. "Oh, it's you."

For a moment I think she's going to keep walking, but she grabs one of the empty beer glasses and carries it to the bar, returning with a wad of napkins.

What is it with me getting soaked with alcohol lately?

I take some napkins from her, wiping at my shirt. "You look good."

The girl in question's hair is curled, and she's wearing heels.

"I'm on a date with a guy I met online. It's not going to work out."

The damp fabric sticks to my skin when I release it. "Sorry."

"Whatever. Are you stalking me?" she demands as I collect the remaining glasses and carry them to the bar.

"I'm here with my roommates and my sister."

"She's the one waking every cat in town?" Madison nods to the stage. "She better not be doing Taylor's Version. Not sure I can handle ten minutes of this."

My lips twitch. "I had no idea you were here. Have you told anyone about Professor Redmond?"

She makes a face. "Haven't had a chance."

The bartender pushes new drinks toward us. I pull out a twenty, but he waves me off. I stuff the cash in the tip jar instead while Madison watches.

"If you talk, they'll keep him from supervising. Which would mean we'd have to forfeit, right after we got through regionals."

"We barely got through regionals. We still have to pass the project justification before winter break."

"I thought that was pretty much guaranteed."

Madison shakes her head. "I heard this year, they're cracking down. They want to filter out even more teams so the top few get more attention in California. If we can't prove our idea will change the world in a real way, we won't get to compete at finals."

This is big. I thought we had a clear path to the finals of Stars, but this is a new roadblock.

"Whatever shit you and Redmond have going on hanging over our heads…" she goes on, "it's not fair, but more than that if what I saw in New York is any indication? It's volatile."

Emma finishes her song and jumps off stage. My roommates clap, and I do too.

"But if you tell," I say under my breath, "don't you think that will screw things up more?"

Madison steps in front of me, expression dark. "Yes. Me telling will mess up everything."

The twisting feeling in my stomach hardens into resolve. "You're right. I put our team at risk by what happened with Professor Redmond. But we can't give up on the Stars competition. We need this."

Her gaze drops to my throat, as if she's remembering what I gave up so we could get through regionals.

"Tell me it's over between you."

Sawyer's grin flashes before my eyes.

His voice, a low murmur for my ears alone.

His thumb stroking under my shirt when he kisses me like everything is right in the world as long as I'm in his arms.

My phone feels hot in my pocket, his unanswered texts burning into my skin as I fight the tightness in my chest.

"We're over."

2

———

SAWYER

"If this is you fixing up the place, you're watching the wrong YouTube videos."

I look up at Daniel, who's standing over me while I rip boards off the porch.

"I figured fuck the flower beds. Time to work on the big things and get this house sold."

The sun beats down, sweat rolling into my eyes.

It's Monday, and for the first time in weeks, I haven't been at the front of a lecture hall, stealing looks at the student who's stolen a piece of me.

I yank the final board off the top, tossing it toward the pile at the end. The nail still embedded in it catches the corner of the house, scratching the wood-work on the windowsill and barely missing the glass.

Daniel coughs and I ignore him.

"Need a saw to get started on the new boards."

He hesitates but then jerks his head across the road.

I follow him that way and into the house.

"You keep your saw in your sunroom?"

"I'm not giving you a saw in this state. You were working on that last night, and you're still there. What's up?"

The room is too small, and I pace the well-worn floors. I'm not a "spill my guts" guy, but he's always been there for me like I've been there for him. And I need to tell someone.

"Olivia's a student."

He rubs a hand over his face. "Shit, Sawyer. I kind of figured, but...shit."

"That's not the problem. She found out what happened in New York this summer."

"All of it?"

"The part where Christina told everyone we were sleeping together."

I was worried sick about Olivia when she didn't meet me, but when she opened the door of her room at the hotel, face twisted with pain and accusation, I knew something was horribly wrong.

When I realized what had happened, that she wouldn't give me the benefit of the doubt, an awful numbness seeped in.

No one ever gave me the benefit of the doubt. Why would she?

Because she was different.

Didn't help that another student walked in on us. But there's no way Madison knows what she saw. If she thinks she does, she's wrong.

"You going to tell her the rest of what happened?"

"I haven't decided."

He grimaces. "Then go. Sell the house and walk away."

"That's the plan."

"Then why do you look as if it's the last thing you want to do?"

Frustration rises up. "I'll leave her thinking this meant nothing. She meant nothing. I know, you're going to tell me I can't feel anything for her."

He turns to a picture of his wife, Andy only a baby in her arms. "Don't turn your back on feelings. You don't know how long you might have with someone."

"Seriously? I was always the 'leap first' one, and you were the 'don't do that, you moron' one."

His neck flexes, the smile not quite reaching his eyes. "Sometimes I look at Andy, and I see his mom, and all I can think about are the ways I should've been better. But the next second I remember I still have him, and I'm grateful. Losing someone you love hurts. But stopping loving once you've started…that's even harder."

"She was your world. This is different."

"You care about Olivia. You can bluster all you want but that doesn't change the fact that it's your feelings that have you running."

I flinch. Everyone in my life has left, and she doesn't owe me anything.

So why does her rejection feel as if someone's digging under my skin with a blunt instrument?

Because every second I spent with her feels like a magic I never let myself believe in.

She's sweet and innocent and smart and brave. I wanted to possess her, to prove there was more to life than she knew. But once I had her, I was the one possessed. Making excuses to see her, to spend time with her, to show her new things.

I shake my head to clear it. "Give me the saw or I'll rent one."

With a sigh, Daniel leads me out to the garage. "You gone through your dad's things yet?"

"The realtor wanted the house cleaned out so she could take pictures. I've thrown stuff in boxes, and I'll move those into the garage this week. Everything except his office."

"That have something to do with it being his favorite place, the one with the most memories?"

"I'm not afraid of ghosts, or memories."

"Right." He gets the saw down off the wall. Instead of letting go when I reach for it, he holds on. "It's an art, Sawyer. Figuring out how you feel. Telling the ones who matter before it's too late."

"Feelings are bullshit. We're judged by our actions."

But as I carry the saw back across the street, I cut a look up at the window of my dad's office.

I head across campus to my office the next morning, twisting the ring on my finger and imagining I can still taste Olivia Barclay on my tongue.

After ripping the deck apart, I found a load of patio stones beneath. Preserved as if they were going to be used then forgotten.

Still thinking over Daniel's comments about knowing what to say to a person after they're gone, I went up to my dad's office to look for a record of the order. I didn't find that, but I found other things.

The receipt for his fish tank and fish.

The bill said to hold for Olivia.

What the hell?

It means nothing.

Except...they were closer than she let on.

She's giving me shit for what happened back in New York, meanwhile she's hiding how well she knew my dad.

There are no classes during fall break, but plenty of people remain on campus. Grad students are working on their projects, plus faculty catch up on research and marking.

Inside the doors of the engineering department, I head up the stairs to the second floor and spin my keys around my finger as I walk to my mailbox. On the way back toward my office, I notice the sign saying the elevator is out of order.

"People can take the stairs," the dean boasts as I'm headed past.

I pull up, thinking of a student in my second-year class who uses a wheelchair to get around campus. "Not all people. Betty," I call to the admin assistant who's walking by. "What's facilities doing on this? Tell them they'll have a lawsuit on their hands."

"Who's going to report us?" the dean asks.

"I will."

His expression transforms from dismissive to irate in a second. I don't stick around to enjoy it.

"Professor Redmond," he calls as I start back down the hall. "I've been meaning to talk to you about a very serious matter. An indiscretion with one of your students."

The hairs on my neck lift, but I force myself to keep walking to the door of my office.

"We were going through some records and security realized Professor Lancaster's keycard was still walking around. Or rather a copy was," he pants as he catches up. "We looked at surveillance of who was entering the building at the same time."

"And?"

His eyes glint. "And it was Olivia Barclay."

The name makes me angry, either because of the way he said it or because hearing it twists the knife in my gut deeper.

"She's a good student. I'm sure it was some kind of error."

I push my door in, but he doesn't get the hint.

"Impossible, and it's in violation of the rules. Don't make excuses for her. Students are adults, capable of making their own decisions and suffering the consequences."

Angry snippets of conversation from years past echo in my mind.

"This is your fault."

"I didn't do anything wrong."

"Then why do these results show you did?"

"Is that what happened five years ago?" I ask, rounding on him. "You made a decision and I suffered the consequences?"

His jaw clenches. "This is a place to learn, Professor."

"I think I've learned all that Russell has to teach me."

"I doubt that very much."

He heads back down the hall without a backward glance.

I'm at the campus bookstore finishing placing a textbook order when awareness prickles my skin under my shirt and jacket.

I turn to spot her scouring the shelves a few feet away.

She's wearing a cashmere sweater a shade lighter than her skin. Her hair is pulled back in a ponytail. The way she's bent at the waist means her skirt rides halfway up her thighs, but it's her profile I'm fixated on—dark lashes, flushed cheeks, parted lips as she searches for whatever prize she's seeking.

She looks new in this light.

"Miss Barclay."

Her head whips around, the ponytail catching her in the face as she straightens. "Sawyer. I mean, Professor."

She's a student.

She's not a woman, not a temptation, not the cause of my fucking heartbeat in my chest.

"I didn't realize you were spending the week on campus." I lower my voice, but there's no mistaking my words.

They're code for "you haven't responded to a single one of my messages."

"After regionals, I don't think we have anything to talk about."

Like hell we don't.

"The dean would disagree with you. You have my father's keycard."

Her eyes widen as if she's not sure if I'm warning her or accusing her.

That makes two of us.

"I had a copy of his keycard. With better permissions. He let me make it."

"Why?"

She doesn't answer.

I pull the receipt from my bag and close the distance between us so I can hand it over, not so I can inhale her scent. "I found this in his office. It has your name written on it."

Once she takes it and reads, there's recognition but no guilt.

"It was my idea to get the fish. I thought he'd like having something in his house to take care of."

If I expect that to make me feel better, it doesn't. My teeth grind.

"You didn't tell me you were close," I say under my breath. "How much time did you spend together?"

"Some." She holds out the receipt. "Why are you so angry?"

Another faculty member walks past me, and I nod at him.

"Because you act like I'm the one keeping secrets," I murmur once we have some space again, grabbing the slip of paper and wadding it in my fist. "But you're the one who lied."

I head back to the engineering building, leaving her and her surprised look.

I never let myself care about anyone and this is why—because they don't stick around when things get hard.

"Maintenance is on the way over to fix the elevator," Betty says at the top of the stairs.

"Good," I grit out.

"Hi, Betty," says a voice behind me.

"Hi, Livvy."

I whirl to see Olivia behind me.

"There is something we need to discuss. Five minutes—Professor," she says.

The hallway feels too short as I head to my office and yank open the door.

She follows me in and shuts the door.

Olivia told me weeks ago that this was my office now. But I'm acutely aware that it's not—it's *his*.

I walk around his desk. Gingerly, I pull open the biggest drawer, as if I'll find some clue about their relationship inside.

Of course, there's nothing.

"Yes, I talked to Madison. Thanks for asking," she says tightly.

"About what?"

"What she saw!"

"She saw nothing. Whatever she thinks she saw, she was mistaken. You and I are the only ones who know what happened, and she's not about to render her hard work redundant on an impulse."

There's a locked drawer above, but no key.

"Are you kidding?" Her voice rips my attention away. "We're this close to being found out, to you losing this teaching job, *another* job"—I flinch—"but you're angry because your dad gave me his keycard? Because I told him he needed a pet?"

I grip the edge of the desktop. She doesn't understand. "Yes."

"Why do people think it's impossible to have

something in common with a person because they're from another generation?" Her brows drag together. "What connects us is shared experience, but it's not as if our lives overlap. It can be a moment—a victory, a hope, a regret. Or a shared emotion. Like a bell ringing that vibrates on a wavelength only certain people can hear. Life is lonely enough, Sawyer. Are you supposed to pretend you don't hear the same bell?"

I've built the wall around my heart one brick at a time until it's high enough to keep everyone out.

Her words slip beneath it.

"How did he make you feel?"

She crosses to his degrees on the wall, studying each as if she's looking at the man himself and not the ink and crests and signatures he worked for. "Like I had a chance to become something."

I want to punch the desk.

"And how did I make you feel?"

Her huff of breath could be humor or frustration or longing. "Like I already was something."

My chest expands.

I'm not my father. Maybe we can get past what happened in New York.

Her gaze drifts to the JENGA set on the corner of my desk. She pokes at one of the bricks near the bottom, causing the entire thing to waver. "But I'm not, at least not to you."

After all the noise and chaos in my head, the silence stretches out painfully.

"When you heard that rumor, how long did it take you to decide it was true?"

Olivia stiffens. "It all made sense. The reason you left New York was some big secret. Add to that the way you pursued me, even after you found out who I was...A lot of men have a thing for younger women."

"Why do you think that is?"

She frowns. "A status symbol? Or if it's secret, I suppose it's a thrill. A reminder of their youth."

"You know what my youth was like. Yet you think I want to be reminded of it."

She folds her arms. "When I asked you in the hallway, you didn't deny the rumor."

Asking. Is that what that was?

It felt like a sentence, handed down from some jury I never met.

My hands form fists behind my back. I want to tell her the truth, but that would make this situation even more dangerous.

"Give me your phone," I say softly.

She hesitates but does.

I hit a few keystrokes, finding what I'm looking for. The breath sticks in my chest as my thumb hovers over the button before I press it.

Warning: This action cannot be undone flashes across the screen.

Confirm.

I pass the device back.

"What did you…" She scrolls through, her jaw dropping. "You erased all of our conversations."

By the time accusing eyes lift to mine, there's no vulnerability. Only anger.

I can see the moment she hates me. The look of loathing is familiar, even if I never expected to see it from her.

"I'm glad he didn't see you like this. You're a judgmental asshole, Sawyer Redmond."

I watch her from the window as she leaves, her high heels clicking down the steps and along the path. It's a reminder of how far out of my reach she is. But I can't stop watching until she disappears.

It's better this way.

The words are less comforting than I expect.

3

OLIVIA

"**I**f you glare at that phone any harder, it's gonna combust."

I look up at Jules from where I'm stretching, one leg extended across the back of the couch, the phone resting on the side table at the end.

"Not glaring. Just...staring. It's all about intent."

"Well, you intend for it to give you back the baby it stole from you. Or something similarly evil," she finishes at my raised eyebrow.

I switch legs and directions, bending over my knee.

He erased our messages.

The conversations starting that first night outside Velvet when he appeared out of nowhere and stole my breath.

The thinly veiled exchanges while we tried to keep our attraction under control.

Then the heat that blossomed after Fall Ball when we stopped denying that he was the man whose face I saw every time I closed my eyes, the man whose touch I dreamed about.

They're all gone, and a part of me is gone with them.

I should erase him from my memories and go back to only being worried about labs and grades and extracurriculars and friends.

After this past weekend in New York, I didn't think I could feel worse.

Except the look on Sawyer's face when he pointed out that I was closer to his dad than I let on wasn't only accusatory, but betrayed.

Maybe I downplayed my interactions with Lancaster because Sawyer knew a different man than I did.

"When you heard the rumor, how long did it take you to decide it was true?"

I want to believe him, because that would make it possible that what we found in stolen moments between classes, in the margins of our life, in the places we were never supposed to meet, was real. That in my flaws and insecurities, he saw not only possibility, but treasure.

A tiny piece of my bruised heart clings to that possibility. I want to be that—real. Ready for the world.

The way he asked the question, as if he's hiding something still, haunts me.

Not that it matters.

He deleted our messages, our entire history, like it meant nothing. He doesn't trust me to keep our secret. He wants to tie up every loose end.

Kat comes out of the bathroom, a hot pink towel wrapped around her. "I have something to help, hang on. I'm working on some new crafts." She starts toward the kitchen, where there's now an entire cooling drawer for sex toys.

"Thanks, but I don't need a distraction. I'm already heading home tonight."

"Since when?"

"Since I realized I left some textbooks there I need for when school starts up again next week."

My phone vibrates on the table.

"You can't stop answering phones," Jules contends. "It's going to be a long, difficult life."

So I reach for it.

"Olivia Barclay please," the woman says.

"This is her," I say.

"We've been trying to reach you but evidently had the wrong contact information. I'm not sure if you're aware, but Albert Lancaster passed a month ago. And he included you in his will."

I press a hand to the vein in my forehead. "You're joking."

"Not a joke."

My hand tightens on the phone, my gaze flying to my roommates.

What? Kat mouths.

"I can't do this right now. I'm sorry," I say, wrapping my sweater around me as I pace the room.

"But—"

I hang up.

"What the hell was that?" Kat asks.

I round to the couch. "Lancaster left me something in his will. I don't know what it is." I picture the shelves of books lining his office. Maybe he wanted me to have some of the volumes he liked pointing to.

"I had a great aunt I never met leave me money," Jules goes on. "It was weird, but she survived a stroke and two husbands and eventually died loaded at ninety-seven surrounded by chihuahuas. I'm not gonna tell her what to do after she's dead."

Kat leans in. "If it's his collection of mothballs, you say a nice prayer for him and toss them in the trash. If it's something good… there are no strings attached."

"But there are strings," I say, flopping onto the couch. "Sawyer won't understand."

Right after I insisted to him we weren't close, it turns out his dad left me something. He'll take it as confirmation that I lied about my relationship with his dad.

I drop the phone on the floor beside me and Jules appears over me, arms folded.

"But if your hot-for-teacher thing is done, why does it matter what he thinks?"

The thought of staring at him three hours a week in class starting Monday, knowing I'll never touch him or kiss him or have him call me Cherry in that tight rasp, is a fresh hell.

"You're right. He doesn't care about me. I was a girl he couldn't have, and a convenient way to get off."

Kat chuckles, and I cut her a look. "What's funny?"

"You're the least convenient way for him to get off." Kat gets that psychologist look in her eyes. "He's gotten a taste of you, and now he's hungry. He's decided he can't get that anywhere else."

It's hard to imagine me as some seductress, but if it is true and I'm a habit Sawyer can't kick...

I bounce off the couch and straighten my clothes. "Then I hope he starves."

The leaves are turning, but as I drive home to New York, they're a blur of red and gold I can't process.

I glance at the texts to my sister.

Liv: How's your week going? Didn't see you in the social posts from the first pep rally of the year.

Emma: That's because I wasn't there.

Liv: ??

There's been no other answer since, and I'm worried about her. She has friends, but no one to look out for her where Mom and Dad are concerned. Emma's cheer captain won't be happy about her skipping the pep rally, and Mom won't be either.

When I get to the townhouse, I breathe in the familiar scent. "Hello?" I call, starting to set my bag on the floor before the habit kicks in that we don't leave things on the floor.

"Olivia. There you are." My dad stalks into the hall, pointing to his tie. "I hate these things and your mother always does them too tight."

I drop the bag long enough to help him with his tie. "What's going on?"

"It's the annual fundraiser for youth services. My firm is a big supporter."

My heart lifts a little. The business must be doing better than it was.

"Your sister's date canceled at the last minute. She had better be ready in half an hour." My mom breezes in, wearing an elegant black sheath dress and fixing on diamond earrings. "It's bad enough we have an extra ticket."

"It might be two extra tickets," my father murmurs.

I finish making the perfect knot and brush past him. My sister's door is shut but there is a pile of fabric in front of it on the floor.

I pick it up to find a shredded skirt, and a top with our high school's team emblazoned on the front.

Still holding the fabric, I knock once on the door before turning the handle.

The room is almost as familiar as my own. All my sister's favorite artsy things around, photos of her with friends, ones with me. One from camp with her covered in paint, which Mom hates. But the grinning girl in those pictures is nowhere in sight.

Emma is sprawled on the bed, her face buried in the pillow.

"Hey. Did I miss some ritual sacrifice?"

She rolls onto her back and takes in what I'm holding with tear-stained triumph.

"I quit cheerleading and Mom freaked out." Emma props up on her elbows, swiping at her face. "She scared off Trey, so I had to retaliate."

"By stopping something you love too?"

She rolls her eyes. "She escalated."

"It's family. Not war."

"Easy for you to say."

Except it's not. Sometimes it feels like negotiating a peace accord. A series of progressive sacrifices in the hope of the kind of acceptance and openness and love other families seem to have naturally.

I shake my head. "Mom said you have a date for the fundraiser."

"Yeah, one she approved of. I called him and told him my herpes was acting up."

I bite my cheek. My sister doesn't lack in the drama department. Act first, think second.

Not unlike Sawyer.

I push that thought from my mind. I'm not letting the man who haunts my thoughts at school follow me home to New York.

"Remember we used to go to this event every year? We'd kick each other and play silent games during the speeches."

She scoots off the bed, heading for the walk-in closet.

Half a dozen cocktail dresses hang in one section of the closet.

She grabs a green one and a pale yellow one and carries them out to drop them on the bed. "Why don't you go in my place?"

I stare at the dresses in surprise. Emma didn't get them out for her, but for me. "My boobs are bigger than yours."

"Way to rub it in." She holds up the green one, tugging at the bodice. "This might work."

I take the dress out of her hands, the satin fabric soft on my skin. "It's obviously yours. You'd look amazing in it."

"Trey thought so too. But now, he won't call me back. I know he's just a guy and it shouldn't matter and I have my whole life ahead of me, but it does."

"I'm sorry, Ems. I know what that feels like." I try not to think of the missing text chain on my phone. A month ago it didn't exist, and now, I'm not sure how I lived before it.

"Emma! You had better be dressed." My mother's voice comes from beyond the door.

My sister's eyes flash, but before she opens her mouth, I cross to the door, opening it a crack.

"Mom, give us a second."

This peace keeping has a familiar chafing, like a pair of shoes that don't quite fit but are too expensive to throw away.

But for the first time in a while, it feels as if my family has a chance for a nice evening together. Emma doesn't think she wants a night out, but she'll stay home and lose herself in feelings if she doesn't.

"I'll go if you take me as your date. It could be fun."

Emma cocks her head. "You want to go?"

"Yeah," I say, honestly. "I do."

It'll feel like a slice of normal after so much craziness.

"And you're going to wear this dress," I declare, pointing to the green one.

"Fine." Her eyes glint before she turns back to her closet. "But I get to pick one out for you."

"She's a Rockefeller who briefly ran off to join the circus as a trapeze artist," I murmur to Emma as we make our way toward the ballroom.

The woman ahead of us wears a long fur with impeccably styled hair. When she turns her head there's the glint of expensive jewelry as her red lips press in a firm line.

"Really?" my sister whispers back. "I thought Anderson Cooper was the last surviving Rockefeller."

"No idea. But the fur is vintage, and there's that 'early capitalist' vibe even though her eyes keep darting toward the exit like she's waiting for her ride."

She laughs and my dad glances over with an absent smile.

"Your mother always put on a brave face about being dragged to these"—she's now trading air-kisses with the woman Emma and I were making up a backstory for—"but I'm glad you girls are enjoying yourselves."

He's in a better mood than the last night we spent together as a family, taking in the basketball game at Russell. But the bitterness barely imprinted on my memory because Sawyer followed me home, made me sandwiches without crusts, and put me back together with his rough hands and patient lips and hooded eyes.

We pass through the entrance to the ballroom, the sign gracing an easel proclaiming that the charity has already raised a million dollars thanks to ticket sales and sponsors.

Several dozen tables with crisp white tablecloths fill the ballroom like a hundred stars. Some are starting to fill in, and we find our way to a table two rows off the stage.

Dad greets business colleagues, shaking hands and trading stories.

"Dibs," Emma mutters, grabbing two seats facing the stage—it's harder to fall asleep with the bright lights. And this way we can see if there's anyone interesting in the front row.

"I'm glad," I tell my dad, leaning over the empty chair he leaves between me and him for Mom.

"About what?"

I lower my voice. "That things are going better. I mean..." I go on at his blank look, "The company must be doing well enough to sponsor a table."

"We could check out the silent auction," Emma interrupts. "You and Mom could use a few days in Italy."

His smile tightens. "I'm sure we don't. Now, you

both look lovely. Let me introduce you to my colleagues."

We make small talk with some business partners of my father's, and moments later, a whisper comes next to my ear.

"Found another. Retired spy, eventually forced to quit because his face was memorable—he looked too similar to the Monopoly man." She points to a short grey-haired man in a tux by an auction table, and I laugh.

"Let's go look. I think I see a turtle sculpture..."

We link arms and head to the side of the room to inspect the long table.

"Oh, it's a real turtle." Emma insists, pointing to the poor creature, preserved by some taxidermist.

"Is that even legal?"

"You can't bring it back to life now. But you could buy it for your apartment."

I cock my head, feeling a pang of sympathy. "Kat and Jules might object."

She takes a sip of her drink. "Why do you think people want animals in their houses?"

I think of Kismet, her eager brown eyes full of love and curiosity. Or Lancaster's jeweled fish, each one with its own drive and habits that together create an entirely unique ecosystem.

"Animals remind us we're no different," I decide. "We can put on designer dresses and drink champagne, but at the end of the day, we're all just fighting to find a place we belong in this world. I can't imagine why someone would want an animal dead."

"Probably the same reason." My attention drags back to the turtle. "If it's a trophy, a symbol that man has conquered all, we can pretend we have control over our lives. Then we're not the animals."

I'm still turning that over as she looks past my shoulder.

"One more. Disgraced royalty, kicked out of the castle for subversive philosophy and sleeping with too many nannies."

I turn and spot the familiar tall frame and slightly rounded shoulders down the row of auction tables. His hair is pulled back from his face, the profile sharp even in boredom as he talks to a man I don't know.

Sawyer.

My stomach knots. The lump rises up my throat until I can't breathe.

"Wait, do I know him?" Emma's words echo in my ears.

Every man in here is wearing a tux, but he's the only one who has this effect on me.

"He's my professor," I manage. "From Russell."

"The one from the basketball game? No way." Emma grabs one of the bidding sheets off the table and fans herself with it. "You look like you could use one too."

I wish I could question why he's here, except of course he is. I'm thinking of him and trying not to, and there's no corner of my life he can't touch with his reckless confidence.

A hand grabs my shoulder.

"Don't do anything," Dad mutters, nodding to the slip of paper in my hand.

"I wasn't going to buy you an island. But"—I take a breath, smiling—"I do want to talk to you about school. Tuition for next semester."

"Unless things change radically, there won't be any next semester."

I blink. "What do you mean? You bought this table for ten thousand dollars."

His smile clicks back into place. "The only reason we're here is to show face and remind everyone we're not bankrupt and hanging our heads in shame."

My face burns.

Things aren't going better. He's clinging to hope by his fingernails.

This isn't a comforting night with family, it's a reminder of how fucked up all of this is.

I force myself to follow my father to our table.

On the way, my gaze lands on the turtle again. This time it's not pity I feel.

It's understanding.

4

SAWYER

I came tonight to rub shoulders with people who could help my new venture with Tate, but also because of promises I made to this charity months ago.

It's a reminder to myself of who I am. My annual gift to this charity has grown every year.

But the second I walked in the door, disdain rose up. Money drips from the chandeliers and every person in this room.

"Take the things you want, Sawyer," my mother used to say with a smile. "No one will offer them to you, even if you're owed them."

When I spot Olivia, I think I'm hallucinating.

But it's not a product of my messed-up head.

Her hair is pinned off one side of her face, sending all those waves tumbling over the opposite shoulder. She's half done up, half wild. She wears a nearly white dress, like a damned angel.

And I'm the devil who made her fall.

When her father grabs her arm and speaks urgently at her ear, every muscle in my body stiffens.

"Tell me you're not having a heart attack," says the tall blond man next to me, his dry tone perfectly matched to the crisp British accent. "You're too young and you don't drink enough."

When Olivia turns to head for her table, I force my attention to my friend. "I should change at least one of those things."

Harrison King might be worth billions but his life was anything but easy. He's an old school friend, like Daniel yet nothing like him at once.

Daniel grew up in a loving home that continues to support him to this day. Harrison had everything, until it was ripped away.

Yet somehow, he's rebuilt himself and his life.

The waiter assigned to our table brings me a gin. We're in the front row near the center and I've chosen a seat on the side of my table.

Harrison takes his seat between me and a twenty-something woman with straight dark hair and full lips. She's wearing a gold dress, but it's her that shimmers.

"Sawyer, this is my fiancée, Raegan."

"The DJ," I say.

"I'm a lot of things, Professor." She leans across Harrison to offer a hand, her eyebrow lifting in amusement. "I'm sure you are, too."

The enormous yellow diamond sparkling on her hand is worn as casually as the clothes.

"Do you always stare at people that intensely?"

She doesn't blink. "I meet a lot of people."

"I'm Harrison's friend with the long hair."

Raegan plays with a fork from her place setting. "I don't remember people by the way they look. I remember them by who they are. We've all got our damage. Might not be easy to see from the outside, but that's what makes someone worth knowing."

I shift in my seat, the hairs lifting on my arms under the tux.

I've been wondering who could've gotten my old friend, the target of every upwardly aspirational woman in the world for a decade, to pledge himself to her.

I get it.

"She's not who I pictured," I murmur to my friend when Raegan turns to speak with the woman on her other side.

"I don't know what I like more. The ways we're similar or the ways we're different."

He slides a hand across the table and flips her

wrist over, threading his fingers through hers without her so much as looking up.

I was prepared to judge her. Instead, I'm envying him.

Fuck. Am I actually jealous of them?

Impossible.

I don't have that kind of faith in love.

But as I shift in my seat and scan the room, I spot Olivia and her family in the next row back.

She looks beautiful and miserable, and if I'm the one who caused that by my actions in my office, I regret it.

But no matter what shit is between her and her parents, it's not my problem.

One of the organizers appears at my arm. "Dr. Redmond. We appreciate your support."

"Is there a change to the introduction?"

"We're not sure it's best for you to speak."

"Because…"

She flinches.

Because I'm a pariah.

I shouldn't care. But there is a lifetime of mistakes that weren't even mine. Strange how society asks us to pay for them.

When I look up, Olivia's watching.

Our gazes lock, and it's like lightning in my brain, thunder in my chest. I didn't expect to see her but it feels inevitable that she's here, witnessing my slow unraveling.

What would it be like to have her sit next to me, like Harrison's fiancée is next to him? To have not only the audacity to be in public together, no matter who cares, but that familiarity?

"I will be making the introductory remarks," I decide, pushing out my chair.

Her eyes fly wide in alarm. "But Dr. Redmond—"

I rise from my seat and head toward the microphone.

"Ladies and gentlemen, welcome to the annual fundraiser for this important charity."

Polite applause fills the room.

"I'm here to introduce the speaker and in a moment I will. But I want to ask how many of you grew up without your biological parents."

A few arms lift slowly.

"Children raised in foster care are underrepresented in this room. And that's how it works. Generosity of the upper class supports those who were born without, but systemic problems reinforce those gaps, and no matter how many dinners we have, we can't fix it. So write your checks, and go home to your beds and sleep soundly, but if you have children, hug them. Tell them they matter. Because one day, you might not be able to."

The room is silent.

A single pair of hands clapping slices through the pause.

I lock gazes with Olivia.

I expect her to be chastising, but she's compassion. Salvation. Forgiveness. All the things I never dared to ask for.

After, it's Harrison who says, "Are you going to introduce me to the woman you can't stop staring at? Because she's coming this way."

She approaches and I clear my throat. "Olivia. This is—"

"Harrison King."

They exchange greetings.

"How do you know Sawyer?" Harrison asks.

If I expect a flicker of nerves in her expression, there is none. "Professor Redmond teaches one of my engineering classes."

"You're lucky to have him."

"He tells us every day."

Harrison snorts and I stare at her over the rim of my drink.

She's teasing me, even here. She's steady where I'm volatile. Light where I'm black.

I curl my hand into a fist to avoid reaching for her.

Olivia departs in a smooth swish of fabric, every bit the elegant swan she played once in *Swan Lake*.

"*Professor Redmond*," Harrison mocks.

I take a long sip of my drink. "Shut up."

Moments later, she's dancing with some guy, and my spine stiffens.

Harrison's words barely make an impact.

"...I'll introduce you to the man I worked with on a club in New York. He's a massive contractor, and..."

I order another drink, my gaze never leaving Olivia.

She listens to what he's saying, but when she smiles, it's forced.

Harrison stares after her. "Let's set aside the fact that you're sleeping with your student—"

"You're the only one who thinks that should be set aside."

"—you don't think you deserve her."

She reaches up to play with her tightly wound hair.

"She might look like some heavenly creature, but she has her share of sins, too."

"She'd be no match for you if she didn't. Take it from someone who thought he knew what he wanted. The right woman doesn't only soften your rough edges. She files a few of them into blades."

Raegan appears from nowhere and Harrison slips an arm around her waist. She murmurs something that makes him grin in a way I haven't seen in years.

Across the dance floor, the guy Olivia's with pulls her closer, his hand sliding down to her ass.

I drain the drink and set it on a tray as I cross to them.

I stop behind her dance partner, making him jerk his head around in surprise.

"You're done here."

"Are you serious?" the guy demands, but when he sees the expression on my face, there's a hint of fear in his eyes.

"Deadly."

He lifts both hands and slinks off into the crowd.

"What are you doing?" Olivia demands, grabbing my arm.

Her touch burns through the jacket and my shirt, has me stepping closer amidst the bodies around us.

"Dance with me."

OLIVIA

I'm staring at Sawyer like he's from another planet.

One full of beautiful, reckless men in tuxedos.

Dance with me.

Is he joking?

"We're in the middle of a fundraiser," I say, my heart accelerating.

His mouth twitches. "If we were in private you'd say yes?"

Damn him.

I shake myself. "No. I don't want to dance with you."

Sure the guy I had been dancing with, the son of one of my mother's friends who's at Columbia, was talking my ear off even before he tried to feel me up.

He also left the second he got a look at Sawyer.

On that stage, Sawyer got up there to prove a point. My parents were appalled by the idea of calling out a room full of rich donors, especially if it required spilling your guts to do it.

It wasn't crude.

It was brave.

"You weren't having a good time with him," my professor says smoothly.

"And you think I'll have a better time with you?" I counter.

"Yes. Because you don't have to pretend with me."

The truth of it vibrates down to my bones.

Tonight, I wanted to enjoy the evening with my family. I was starting to believe this life wasn't so bad

—until my dad reinforced this is all an act, and my future rests in the balance.

The only person who's not acting here is the man in front of me.

Sawyer's waiting for me to respond and now, with the music and the darkened lights and everything that's happened tonight, I force the words from my lips. "We can't do this."

"Here or at all?" He steps closer.

"Both."

But his palm is warm and rough as it clasps mine. "Noted."

I place my other hand on his shoulder. The wool suit strokes my fingers.

Sawyer is possessive without grasping. His entire countenance draws me closer.

I try to take a steadying breath but when I do, I breathe him instead of oxygen.

We're surrounded by the very people we've tried to hide from.

I'm a butterfly trapped in a box, a panicked display. If any onlooker could feel how fast my heart is kicking against my ribs, they'd know this is more than it looks like.

"You've been drinking gin," I murmur.

"It's for special occasions."

"Entertaining assholes?"

He chuckles, the sound warming me everywhere.

The song seeps into my brain, and it takes a moment to recognize it: an orchestral version of "Perfect."

"I love this song," he murmurs.

My throat is a desert. "A closet Ed Sheeran fan. Full of surprises."

"Don't you get it by now? I'm not your typical professor. These people are hollow pretenders who care more about looks than substance."

I want to press my face to his lapel, or better yet, his neck. "What do you care about?"

His touch strokes up my back. "You."

It's one word, forced.

It cuts bone deep.

"You shouldn't."

"That's when I care the most."

I rip out of his hold, catching his startled expression before I spin on my heel and take off for the hallway.

Dodging bodies in the dark, I try not to run until I shove through the ballroom doors.

Outside, I start down the corridor, my heels catching on the carpet. I don't know where I'm going, but I need space to breathe that's away from my family, the posturing, the pretending, but also away from Sawyer.

There's a potted tree and I duck behind it.

It's only moments before my privacy is torn in half.

Sawyer shoves between me and the wall, forcing my chin up.

"Is it that terrible being close to me?" His handsome face fills my vision, his tie at an angle as if he was yanking on the fabric. "You didn't used to hate it."

"You can get up on stage and rip into those people because you don't need them. But this is my life, Sawyer. You can't tell me to stand up for myself and everything will be okay. Because you don't understand, and you gave up the right to care."

"Tell me anyway."

My eyes are burning. "My family's splintering apart, my dad's business is crashing down and he's trying to hold it together but he doesn't believe in his own daughter. Everything I thought I knew is crumbling. And you're the one who made me see the cracks."

Sawyer grabs my shoulders, his fingers digging in until my flesh hurts. "Olivia..."

I shove him, hard.

He trips backward a step before straightening. His steady hands adjust his shirt collar.

"Again. Come on, sweetheart."

I do, not because of the invitation but the endearment.

How dare he care?

He deleted our texts, our history, our relationship.

We aren't anything.

This time, he hits the wall.

A rainbow of emotions—concern, regret, something that makes his eyes gleam—are scrawled across his face, and my heart skips.

His gaze drops to my throat for a beat, two.

Then he tucks my head under his chin and wraps both arms around me.

Out there, the world is fucked but everyone pretends it's not.

Here in Sawyer's arms…there's no hiding. There's only truth and strength.

His fingers play with my hair. He leans his forehead against mine, holding my face with both hands.

He smells like alcohol but every part of me aches to beg him to hold me again, to tell me everything will be fine, to blanket me with his reckless confidence.

"You said you're not what people expect. So what are you?" My breath trembles between my lips.

His eyes lighten, honey tones dancing in the dark chocolate. It should soften him.

It doesn't.

"A man who hates himself almost enough he can't sleep at night, but not enough to stay away from you."

I squeeze my eyes shut against the traitorous thudding of my heart.

We could get out of here. Run for the street, deal with the consequences later.

It's even harder than I expect to pull away when he's holding me. "I need to get back."

I return to the ballroom, checking my makeup in my compact mirror on the way.

"Nice hair," Emma says as I retake my seat.

It's not until I feel the side of my head that I realize Sawyer took all the pins out.

5

———

SAWYER

"**W**hat?" I bark as the speaker in my Mercedes' notifies me of an incoming call.

"Sawyer, it's Tate. Apologies for missing the fundraiser. I heard there were some top partner prospects there."

"You mean suits with more money than brains? Sure. Give them chandeliers and open bars, they're good to go."

Now that I'm on my way back from the city, I'm glad Tate wasn't there. If he'd come, he would've seen a man consumed by thoughts of a woman.

After Olivia left me in the hallway last night, I returned to the ballroom for the requisite glad-handing. But my head was only half in it.

The only future I cared about was one that

involved wiping away her tears until I could make her laugh, reminding her with my lips and words and body that she's enough and it'll all work out.

I wanted to help her, in my own fucked up way, but instead I made things worse.

"Your remarks seem to have made an impact." Tate's voice cuts into my thoughts.

"It was an introduction."

"We need to be careful not to piss people off."

"Is that why you called?"

"No." He sighs. "Talent acquisition. If we're going to start our new firm as scheduled, we need hires."

"We are the talent. Look at the top companies in any industry; what's lacking is vision, not manpower. Steve Jobs revolutionized communications, not an army of yes-men."

"I'm not talking about yes-men, I'm talking about engineers. Ten at least to get us started. You can't do all the work—you don't have the time or the expertise." He pauses. "I'm guessing this was part of the problem at your old company."

"The problem at my old company was my cofounder was severely limited in his ambition. Graham cared more about the bottom line than pushing the frontier."

My gaze drops to the stone watch on my wrist, a

stark contrast to my ex-cofounder's shiny oyster Rolex.

"It's not either-or, Sawyer. We need to keep the lights on and pay the bills. Being the first mover is hard and expensive. The second mover, the one who follows close behind, gets the spoils."

"But he has to look himself in the mirror at night and know that he was second." I let that sink in. "We'll get people from your firm. You're a Senior Vice President for fuck's sake."

"They won't walk without the assurance of a bigger payday."

"I can try to interest people from my former firm. There are a few who might move with us. I'll make some calls."

After hanging up with Tate, I pull over to the side of the road and find my contact list from the old company.

Thirty minutes later, I've spoken with three former colleagues. None of them expressed more than a vague interest in moving.

This is a problem.

I click off and shove a hand through my hair as the road flies past my window.

I wanted a fresh start with a former rival, making the best tech on the planet. The rush of living on that edge, having money for R&D, not watching my ass or worrying about who else is.

Now, we need to attract new talent, too. I mentally scroll through names in my class roster. I know their faces, but next to nothing about their lives.

I don't know who they are, or what they want.

When I get back into town, I don't bother stopping at home but go straight to campus and up to my office.

I pull up my dad's academic files from past years. He used to assign a short paper on why students wanted to be engineers. Sure enough, I find most of my students in there—including Madison, Royce, Adam, and Olivia.

My cursor hovers over the last one, but in the end, I ignore it and open the others.

If Tate and I are going to be able to recruit a team to support the work we're planning to do, one of us needs to be able to bring junior engineers on staff and mentor them once they're there.

I should've spent less time thinking of Olivia and more thinking of the rest of them.

That changes today.

OLIVIA

Liv: Can I get today's class notes from you?

Adam: Sure. But you owe me ;)

The first Monday after fall break, I skip engineering class.

Cowardly? No. I have other shit to get done before meeting the team in lab and I don't need to face Professor McHottie on top of it.

In my last fifteen minutes of history, I'm flipping through my notebook when I find my note I made a few weeks ago.

. . .

How to be a badass:

    1. Date who I want. (And not who I don't.)

2. Pursue my own career and personal interests.

3. Become financially independent.

So the first one's easy. I'm not dating anyone.

But I am pursuing my own interests, and if our team can win this competition, it'll set me up for a legitimate career.

Still, there are problems. Big ones.

This afternoon is the first team meeting since break, and I haven't talked to Madison except our run-in at the bar a week ago.

I hoped to arrive early to corner her, but our history prof ends the day by announcing the midterm time, which conflicts with one of my labs, so I stay late to plead my case.

As I head across campus, the late afternoon sun has me stripping off my sweater. The pleated skirt and tank top are cute for class but less than ideal for actually working. But I don't have a second to head home and change like I'd planned.

At least Sawyer won't be there. Today, I'm grateful not to have to face him.

I've always liked the engineering design lab. It's not the lab itself, but what goes on there: projects, creativity, exploration of ideas.

I run into Adam on the way in.

"You're here early," I comment.

"Madison suggested getting a head start."

I'm immediately on alert.

She changed her mind and she's planning to tell them about me and Professor Redmond.

"Missed you over break," he says. "A few of us went to a party at Keaton's."

I focus on his words and not the feeling of impending doom. "Remember when you broke that vase of his mom's back in senior year when you were high and throwing it around like a football?"

"I thought I was a dead man." He shakes his head.

"You get away with everything. It's that smile."

The smile in question appears. "Everything okay? Your mom skipped lunch with mine, and when you texted to say you weren't coming to class, I wondered if something was up."

Adam puts his hand on the small of my back, and I step forward. "Yeah. We're doing okay."

"Liv..."

I cut him a look. "It's been a little stressful with my dad's work, and Emma."

"I'm here for you. You know that, right?"

His eyes search mine, looking genuinely concerned.

And as much as he was a dick earlier this semester, he does understand what my world is like because it's his world, too.

We make our way into the lab to find Madison's already there, facing a whiteboard, plus Royce, but it's the third figure between them that has my chest tightening.

Sawyer's wearing a black T-shirt over jeans and boots. His hair is tied back and he writes on a whiteboard.

A dull object pokes my stomach and I curse as I run into the corner of a lab table.

Adam grabs me, a hand on my waist and another on my shoulder. "Easy there," he laughs. "Need me to carry you to lab? Cuz I'll do it."

All three of them turn this way.

Our professor's gaze flickers over me and Adam, making every inch of my skin tingle.

"Glad you guys could make it," Madison says. "We're going over the schedule for the rest of the semester and we started brainstorming what we can improve on after regionals." She motions to the whiteboard.

"Since when does Professor Redmond come to meetings?"

Royce arches a brow and Madison blinks at me.

"Since now," Sawyer replies, a warning lurking just below the surface.

"Go with it, Liv." Adam laughs at my side. "We're getting extra help, it's a good thing."

"This is just a team meeting," Royce says, crossing to us. "It's still a long road to nationals and we can't do it without him."

He's right. I should focus on being the team leader they can trust, the one who pulls her weight.

I glance at Sawyer and take a deep breath. "Sure. No problem."

An hour later, Sawyer's been less watchful mentor than drill sergeant. He's been giving us all kinds of menial tasks. Wires and circuit components are scattered across the lab counter, none of which are attached to the robot.

"Are you sure we need to practice this kind of circuitry? We're not going to use it." Royce holds two wires up to the light.

"If this robot is going to be able to function in a

range of environments and be small enough to fit in a modest space, you need flexibility."

"Listen, we just need to build a thing that gets the judges off, yeah?" Adam gripes, nodding to the robot. "A little refinement and it can jack you off, Professor."

Madison groans and I rub a hand over my face.

"Not my type, but thank you, Adam."

Royce frowns. "We're here to design something that could change the world."

Adam looks at all of us. "And by that they mean make cash."

"Or you could do something that actually makes a difference." We all turn toward Sawyer. "Everything we design starts with a vision of what could be. A future that's different than the present we're living in. You could try to make everyone's world better, not only your own."

My heart thuds against my ribs. It's as much as I told him before at Fall Ball.

"And before you forget, there's an important call to discuss the requirements for the next phase of the submissions. I assume you'll all be there enthusiastically taking notes," he continues.

Groans go up. "It's midterms," Royce sighs.

Madison shakes her head. "Whatever, we'll be there."

But I step forward. "It's okay. I'm the team lead, I'll take care of it."

"You're the best." Adam reaches out to tuck a piece of hair behind my ear before I can stop him.

I don't look at Sawyer, but I feel his attention scorching my skin.

"And you're out of materials." Sawyer nods to Adam. "You can head to the supply room to get more."

It's grunt work but Adam doesn't blink. He's probably happy for a reprieve, and to stretch his legs. "Need your pass, Professor."

"It's okay. Mine has enhanced permissions. I'll go too." The words are out before I think to stop them. The reason mine has enhanced permissions is because Lancaster made them that way, which is a sore spot for Sawyer. But I hop off the counter where I'm seated.

"You think you two can find it?" Royce says. "No hooking up in the supply room."

Adam laughs.

Sawyer's heavy stare settles on my back until we're out the door.

"Seriously. As if we can't do basic electrical engineering without having to practice," Adam starts as we head down the hall. "This is where you say 'you're imagining things, Adam, he has our best interests at heart.'"

I snort. "He's punishing us. Something crawled up his ass and he's taking it out on us."

Adam's laughter echoes off the walls.

We find the room and swipe my pass by the door.

The design lab supply room is its own warehouse, more than a dozen rows lined with shelves and drawers of computer chips and LEDs, microcontrollers and wires. There are boards and chips and tools and soldering equipment.

It's a dream, or it would be if someone kept on top of organizing it.

We go to different aisles in search of the components we were sent here for.

A moment later, I'm pressed up against one of the shelves by a very hard, very angry professor.

"What are you doing?" His voice is a rasp, his body taut and distracting as his best parts line up with mine.

"Sourcing a bunch of bullshit my professor sent me to find." I cock my head. "Wanna help?"

His eyes are dark, his lips thin. "I didn't send you. I sent him."

"And why is that? Because I'm on speaking terms with Adam?"

"According to you it's because something crawled

up my ass."

Shit. Of course he heard that.

"It's not my ass you should be worried about," he finishes, and my eyes narrow.

"If you want to help the team, help us. We don't need to be lectured at, and we don't need to build circuits until our fingers are cut."

"Hey, Liv? You find the stuff on your half of the list?" Adam calls.

"Working on it!" I call back.

Sawyer moves closer. His hand is gripping my right arm, tugging me against him. "I'm not here to play games, Olivia."

"Really? Because I'm here to work on a project that's going to determine my future. Your presence is optional."

We stand motionless for a moment, and my heart is racing. I push on his chest but he's not moving. He grabs my other wrist and pulls me so close that I feel his breath on my neck.

"My father left you a sum of money. A very generous sum of money."

"I have no idea what you're talking about."

"The attorney said she called you before the gala, which you failed to mention when we saw one another. Apparently you thought you could hide that little fact from me."

So that's what this is about.

The truth that I had no idea is on the tip of my tongue, but I swallow it.

"You're right," I retort. "I wanted his money. I was hoping he'd die and leave me a bunch of cash."

"Stop it. You're being a brat—"

"I didn't know he had a son, but given what he left me, clearly I was better to him than his own child ever was."

His face goes white.

I've struck a nerve. In this man who claims to care about nothing, I've snuck beneath his defenses and hit him where it hurts.

Regret slams into me. I wanted a reaction from him, but not this one. I'm about to take it back when Adam's voice interrupts from a few rows away.

"Liv, I think I found it." He's far too close for how our professor is currently boxing me against the shelf, chest heaving. "But I need to go get one more thing on the list. It says there's stock here but I don't see any. I'm going to check in the supply closet, maybe it got moved there."

Sawyer and I stare each other down until I hear the click of the door.

My throat works. "I didn't mean—"

"I don't want your apology." He turns away and the moment his touch is gone, I miss it.

"Then what do you want, *Professor*? What makes us even?"

Because no matter what's between us, there's no excuse for what I said to him.

Sawyer is being a jerk but I wasn't playing fair. He brings out a side of me that's impatient and needy and angry and vulnerable.

"You mean it." His eyes flash.

"Anything." My pulse thuds in my throat, but I'm not afraid of him. "You want to punish me, do your worst. But when we walk out of here, we're on level ground."

What I'm afraid of is that he's going to leave and I'll lose him forever.

We're trapped in a hopeless cycle. I can't have him, I shouldn't want him, but I still do, and maybe he feels the same way.

In the tension of his body, the clench of his jaw, I want to believe he gives a shit. I want to believe he cares.

He turns it over and I see the moment he decides.

He pulls me to a low file cabinet at the end of the aisle. "Bend over."

"If you want more lace to jerk off with, you can go to Victoria's Secret and buy it yourself."

His low chuckle lifts the hairs on my arms. "This time, it's not fabric I'm taking."

If he's not stealing my underwear again, then what...

I do as Sawyer asks, folding at the waist and lying there, the cool surface of the cabinet against my face.

"It's not my ass you should be worried about."

My body throbs, reminding me he hasn't touched me in more than a week.

Is it messed up that part of me wants him to fuck me right now? That as much as I want to walk out that door, I want him to spread my thighs and sink into me from behind, his possessive hands holding me open and his raw groan at my ear?

Sawyer flips up my skirt and I feel my bare cheeks in the open air.

If his heavy exhale is a warning, his words are an alarm.

"Have you ever been spanked?"

The breath trembles between my lips, heat curling low in my stomach. "No."

I'm afraid now.

Not of the pain. But every time we do something new, it leaves a mark on me I can't wash away.

He might be angry with me but he's turned on, too. It's a kind of power—the only one I have.

It's not. I can leave.

But if I do, I shut a door I'm not prepared to close.

Because part of me still hopes for him. For us.

"You took advantage of my trust. There are consequences."

His trust. Those two words make my heart kick.

He did trust me, if only a little. He did let me in, if only for a moment.

He sets his watch on the cabinet next to my face, the second hand ticking silently.

"One minute. You last, we're done for today. The team can go home."

He's giving himself a time limit to break all the rules. Even the ones he hasn't broken with me already.

"Unless you're tapping out," he finishes.

It's one minute.

One minute to see if there's something here I missed. Sort the truth from the lies, the ones he told me and the ones I told myself.

One minute to silence both our judgments and feel the connection that's always been real between us.

The stakes have never been higher, and it's not only because Adam could come back at any time.

"I'm not tapping out."

I said I'd play. But Sawyer has to start.

The first smack lands on my right ass cheek.

It's sharp. I yelp, more in shock than in pain.

I brace myself for another, focusing on the stinging spot on my skin that seems to spread with each moment.

But the second smack comes on the other side.

My fingers dig into the cabinet. This time, I swallow my sounds.

"You asked for this, Cherry."

Is he reminding me or himself?

The pain fades but doesn't disappear. There's a matching throbbing on both sides of my butt.

The second hand on the watch is barely past the two.

It feels like I can earn his trust.

Earn *him*.

He adjusts my thong, tugging up to give him more of a canvas.

My core throbs as the fabric pulls tight across my flesh. My thighs clench together, but the tug of desire is only a momentary distraction when his hand comes back down.

He's spanking me hard now, loud smacks that echo through the room.

My skin is on fire.

The second hand seems to slow down as it rounds the four. The six.

I can't do another thirty seconds of this.

Right when I'm about to call him off, his hand returns, squeezing and then rubbing, soothing the pain.

My back arches and a tiny sigh slips out.

I'm confused. It hurts and then it doesn't. It's awful and then beautiful.

"Are you enjoying this?" His whisper is so low it's barely audible.

Is he reading my mind or my body?

The rasp of his breathing says it's affecting him every bit as much as me.

I twist and look up at him, my eyes burning.

His pupils are blown, but instead of looking open and exhilarated, he's closed off.

Sawyer isn't reckless and free-spirited. He's wired to judge and condemn. He might be open when it comes to sex, but when it comes to trust, he's jealous and stingy.

So when does it end?

The answer's obvious. *Never.*

"Stop."

His entire body recoils. He flips my skirt back down and steps back.

"I thought that this would make us even," I start. "But it isn't even about me. You're getting off on punishing the world that screwed you over. I didn't take the money," I go on before he can respond. "I didn't even know there was money. The lawyer called me but I hung up before she could tell me the details."

I adjust my clothes while he watches with dawning horror.

"I never wanted to take from you. I wanted to meet you on level ground. Or as level as we could be given the circumstances." I smooth my skirt down, wincing as my skin burns. "But I see now that will never happen, because you won't ever let anyone in. So forget it, *Professor*. I'm done trying to earn anything from you."

His dark eyes pin mine, and I refuse to be drawn in by the emotions in them. "Olivia—"

"I couldn't find it." The click of the door opening is lost in the sound of Adam's voice. "Redmond's going to have to go get it himself if he wants it so badly," he says, rounding the corner.

He looks between us and I swipe at the corner of my eyes before he can spot my tears. I take a step toward him, behind him.

"You're looking for this?" Sawyer reaches over to the shelf next to us and holds up the piece Adam was searching for.

Adam blinks, sheepish. "Oh. I must've missed it before."

When the three of us walk back to the lab together in silence, I stick close to Adam.

This time, I don't feel Sawyer's eyes on my back.

I don't think he's looking at me at all.

7

SAWYER

"Would you like cream?" the barista asks.

"No. Black."

The coffee lands in front of me, the color warm like caramel.

"Shit, you said black, didn't you? It's been a rough morning." She grimaces. "I'll remake it."

I hold up a hand. "It's fine."

"It's not, you asked for black—"

"I used to drink it with cream in school. I'll get over it." I force a smile and turn with my light-tinted coffee to head toward the back.

I pass the handful of occupied tables, a mix of town dwellers and Russell U students gossiping and studying at Some Like It Hot, a popular café that's new since I was last in town.

What's with the nice guy act?

I'm feeling guilty over what went down at the supply room. It was a new low. Not an emotional one, but a moral one.

This morning, I met Daniel for a run. It felt good to work out my arms and legs and get my blood pumping. But every footfall on the pavement had me thinking about Olivia.

What we had before last week: the way she melted in my embrace, how she kissed me back, how she opened up to me so easily.

Then the way she looked at me after she straightened her clothes in the supply room.

Finding out my dad left her fifty grand, I couldn't see straight. Not because of the money but because it meant that he cared about her. And knowing her, she cared about him.

Hearing her and Adam joking in the hallway broke the last of my control.

I bent her over a cabinet and reddened every inch of her ass for how she made me feel, including the cheap insults she hurled my way once we were alone.

I'd only meant to shock her a little but I got carried away.

When I was done, she looked up at me with

those stubborn dark eyes full of accusation and said she didn't even take the money.

What I couldn't say was it punished me as much as her.

I sink into a seat, setting my notebook on the table.

Maybe there is something wrong with me.

I can blame my father all I want, but there was a sliver of darkness in my heart before I ever met Albert Lancaster, and it outlived him.

I pull up the student essays I started reading the other day, but the ringtone on my phone interrupts before I get far.

"Sawyer," my former partner says.

"Graham. So you've finally called to offer me my half of the company back."

"It seems as if you're trying to take it." A pause. "One of our junior engineers said you've been asking who's interested in moving."

"Did you expect me to deny it? I don't deny facts."

"I didn't call to discuss what happened last year."

There's an old *New York* magazine on the windowsill from whoever was here last, and I thumb through the business news. I stop when I see a piece about both of us.

"Can you even look her in the eye?" I drawl. "If I

had a daughter I put up to lying to the entire world like you did, I sure as hell couldn't."

When we founded the company five years ago, it was a balance of client work and our own projects—the former paid the bills. But it was always our aspiration to do more cutting-edge development.

The tension came to a head last year when I decided to allocate a few million in budget to new projects without proven markets yet.

He said no. Like the company wasn't half mine, too.

I pointed out he was stuck in the past, like every other firm in New York.

So instead of dealing with it man to man…

He set a trap.

One there was no hope of avoiding.

The day after, the entire staff looked at me like they weren't sure what kind of man I was.

I'm the ruthless kind. The reckless kind.

When the world doesn't care enough, you have to look out for yourself.

"Stay away from our talent," Graham warns.

"The talent we built."

"The talent I built. You were never a team player. That was your downfall, and continues to be your legacy."

"And you tethered yourself, our company, and

every one of its employees to the past. That will be yours."

I click off, tossing the magazine back on the windowsill.

A set of four files I emailed to myself sits in my inbox.

The student essays. The three I read were predictable. Family legacy. Industry reputation. Becoming the first person with a professional degree.

There's one I didn't open yet.

Olivia's.

It felt like invading her privacy.

But yesterday threw me. She's not going to speak to me, yet I need a piece of her. She wrote this for my father, to him. I want to see her like he did.

Now, here in public, I open the essay.

I wanted to be a dancer for as long as I can remember. Most people think ballet is glamorous; it beautifies graceful women and men. When I tied the ribbons on my pointe shoes, it felt like I was going to war. I put my body through hell for a kind of competence. I thought my work would be rewarded, but it wasn't. Because merit only counts for part of it.

They told me I couldn't be a dancer when I was seventeen. I was crushed. I wish I could say I didn't remember that time, but I remember every hour of every day. It was dark. I dragged myself to school, went through the motions, until we had a project to build a circuit board. It gave me something to focus on. I discovered science.

That's what I love about designing and building. If you do everything right, you can win. No one can stop you. Science won't stop you. Laws of thermodynamics and electricity don't care about your face or your arches or your body weight or your parents. It's a place I can belong.

And instead of helping it be hers, I'm standing in her way.

"Can I get you another coffee?"

I shut the screen of my notebook. I feel like someone's punched me in the gut.

I blink up at the waitress, my throat tight. I shake my head and she leaves.

Maybe Graham's right about one thing, and I did care too much about myself.

Conversation from the counter streams into my consciousness. A familiar female voice.

"...The defensive line was a letdown. I told those boys to shake off whatever's going on and get their heads on straight."

I turn in my chair to find Betty leaning over the counter talking to the barista.

"Sawyer?" She grabs her to-go cup and heads this way. "You tried the oat milk lattes in this place?

Thing of beauty. Like our nemesis' tackle last weekend."

She drops into the chair opposite without an invitation, adjusting to get comfortable in the worn leather seat. "Honey, what's eating you?"

"Did my father have close relationships with many of his students?"

Betty frowns. "I wouldn't say close. Why?"

I rub a hand over my neck. "The dean said a student had a copy of his keycard to get into rooms."

"Everyone does it, Sawyer. Who're you thinking of?"

"Olivia Barclay. He spent time with her."

"I know you're used to looking for the worst in people. You can blame the dead all day long; they don't have the breath to argue. But don't you blame anything on that girl. Because she's a doll and I will use more than my breath to set you straight." Her eyes shine. "Now what else can we solve today?"

I've fucked my student and can't seem to stop, even when she won't let me touch her.

"My future business partner and I are trying to recruit students. Evidently it's not enough to simply offer someone a job these days."

"Students want to know an invitation is personal, specific. They want to feel like they matter."

I rub a hand over my neck. "So I buy them all

birthday cakes? Send them participation ribbons for deigning to take my class?"

She laughs. "In the last few years your father agreed to take on more service activities, like supervising the student projects, helping with the engineering club. I think that endeared him to them."

"I'm already doing Stars, though I may have fucked that up."

But Olivia was wrong when she said I was making them jump through stupid hoops.

I wanted to see what they were made of. School has a way of filling your mind without preparing you for the real world. That's one gift I can give them. The doctorate I have in engineering is nothing compared to the one in life.

"You could try something truly radical to convince them you care." Betty's eyes shine.

At this point, I'll try anything.

8

———

OLIVIA

When I sink gingerly into my seat in calculus, my hands balled into fists, I look good.

It's a lie. I'm a damned mess.

My fingertips are sliced from working with wires in lab, and my ass is complaining.

It feels as if there's an imprint of Sawyer's hand on my flesh.

There probably is.

Sixty seconds indeed.

I'm sure it was his intention that I wouldn't forget for long after I walked out the door, and he got his wish.

Whatever. I'm over it, and him. He has bigger problems than I can solve, and yesterday proved it.

My phone vibrates with a call—the number of

the attorney, probably following up about the inheritance.

I could use the money. If what my dad said at the gala is true, I can't rely on my parents. And I'm sure Lancaster would be satisfied to see it go to that purpose.

Plus, it's none of Sawyer's business. And as far as I'm concerned, neither am I.

Royce and Madison walk in the door, engrossed in conversation, and I shove the phone into my bag.

Royce spots me and comes over. Madison trails him, looking like she'd rather sit anywhere else but drops into the seat on his other side.

"You finish the homework?" he asks.

"Barely. You?"

"Most of it." He grins and Madison rolls her eyes.

"That's because you can't stop playing NBA games on your Xbox."

"Adam's into those too. He's really good."

"Huh. I'll have to challenge him sometime." He pulls out his books. "Speaking of Stars, having Professor Redmond supervise is turning out great."

I frown. "Were you part of the same lab session we all were in?"

"Yeah, but he sent me this email today. Asked what I wanted to do after school and gave me some options."

All he gave me was a red ass.

"He's kind of a genius," Royce continues, oblivious. "He won all these awards here and at grad school, and he's got more than two dozen patents."

"I get it. He's God's gift to undergrad engineering," Madison intervenes.

"That's just it. He doesn't have to be here. When he left his company, he made a lot on the deal. When I got into Russell on financial aid, I knew I'd get a good degree. I didn't expect an experience like this. Now it feels like we have a real chance to make nationals for Stars. With that, plus a reference from Redmond, I'll be able to go anywhere."

I'm not the only one moved by Royce's passion. Madison's watching him, swept up.

"Is that why you wanted to sit with me?" I tease. "So you can gush about Professor Redmond?"

"No, I came to sit with you because I found something in the lab that I think belongs to you."

He reaches into his bag and pulls out his fist.

Inside it is my necklace.

The diamond pendant glitters in the light. My stomach drops, disbelief blurring with gratitude.

"I found it at the end of the day. It looked familiar so I didn't turn it in right away, then I remembered you wearing one like it. Is it yours?"

I lift it, inspecting the diamond, the clasp. Every-thing is perfectly intact.

"Yes," I murmur. "But..."

I traded it at regionals in New York to another team in exchange for materials to fix our robot.

Madison knows that, too, but Royce doesn't.

"Thanks," I manage.

I grip the solitaire in one hand, still not believing it's here.

How did it come back? I can't believe one of the guys on the other team had a change of heart.

Which leaves one other option.

I fasten the necklace around my throat, the familiar feel of it pure comfort as I type out a text.

Liv: I don't know how you did this, but thank you.

The response comes moments later.

Adam: For what?

"Miss O!" Sienna, one of the little girls in my guppies class, screeches as I wind my way across the studio. "Andy cut me off."

The boy in question looks around, confused. "Did not. We're supposed to go this way."

"You're supposed to go the other way," Sienna argues.

I'm teaching dance and enjoying the six- and seven-year-olds. They're doing a liberal interpretation of chassés around the perimeter and they're so cute, I'd watch them even if I wasn't getting paid.

"Let's all go to the right this time"—I motion with my hands—"and we can go to the left next time."

This time, the kids go to the right...except for Andy, who steps on Sienna's toes.

"He did it on purpose!" she cries.

"Did not!"

"People make mistakes. It's good to forgive them."

"What if I don't want to?"

"Well, we can spend the rest of class talking about whose fault it is, or we can talk about what's next once we master this."

The screeching stops. "What's next?" Sienna asks.

"Well, then we can add a kick." I relevé onto my left foot and bring my right up in a développé, extending it at waist height to the side.

"Then what?"

I back into the corner and take a breath.

I do a chassé into a jeté, landing easily and resetting to execute a triple pirouette in place.

"Wow." Murmurs go up.

The movements linger in my body, the tension and the extension. Like a friend I haven't seen in too long, the kind who makes you feel instantly at ease despite the distance.

"But that's next week," I joke. "One more time around the studio, then we'll finish for today." I ruffle their hair and encourage them to get back to work.

I feel his eyes on me before I can turn toward the windows looking into the studio.

He stands on the other side of the glass, heavy gaze locked on me like I'm the cause of every good and bad day he's ever had.

After the time is up, I escort my kids toward the door.

"And I thought my classes were contentious," Sawyer murmurs.

I refuse to smile. He doesn't deserve it. "Guess I almost threw down with the asshole that one time. You're here for Andy?"

"Daniel's in the parking lot. I'm here for you."

It's impossible not to be affected. The way he says those words makes my heart race.

His gaze drops to the necklace around my throat and my chest expands.

"It was you, wasn't it?"

Sawyer's eyes darken as if he's about to deny it.

"I knew it was important to you."

"But when…"

"At regionals, before we were supposed to meet up."

Before we fought in the hallway.

Before Madison caught us.

He did that for me.

"Looks better on you than the kid you traded it to anyway," he says with a grimace.

"So what is this? An apology?"

"No. That's a gift. This is the apology." He takes a breath, looking so awkward I almost feel for him.

Almost.

"You were right. I like to hold people at a distance. After regionals you pushed me away, and finding evidence of you and my father in each other's lives…I hated that he got to have you when I didn't."

And I got to have him, I think but don't say.

The words are a big concession.

They're not enough.

"Apologies usually contain the words 'I'm sorry.' For instance," I press before he can interject, "I'm sorry if me keeping anything from you about your dad hurt you. That's exactly why I did, and it backfired."

He looks around the studio, his jaw working. "In that case..." his voice lowers even though all the kids and parents are out of earshot. "When I punished you in the supply room, I was angry, and you didn't deserve it. I'm sorry."

"You should be. I couldn't sit comfortably all day," I grumble.

I realize my mistake the second his hands flex at his sides. "Really. I can take a look if you like."

"Hard pass. Forget I said anything."

"Like I said. Very, very sorry." His eyes gleam with banked desire and amusement.

"Sure you are." I grab my dance bag, realizing too late the zipper's open and spilling the contents onto the floor.

"I read your essay. The one you turned in to my dad last semester."

"You what?"

On my knees, I pick up my street clothes, spare leotard, wallet, and stuff them back inside.

"I don't want to stand in the way of you getting what you want." Sawyer's next to me, too close as he helps. "I want you to have all of it."

He means Stars, but I want what I felt in his arms, under his touch.

But I can't go there with him again, because of what I told Madison and because it would be destructive to let him in the way I was starting to. He didn't only claim my body, he had a piece of my heart.

And he wrecked it.

"It's better if we focus on school." I rise to standing and he follows.

"So you'll sit in my class, dutifully taking notes, pretending you can't remember how I make you come."

My skin prickles everywhere, a dull ache settling between my thighs.

"That's exactly what I'll do." I start to turn away, using every ounce of willpower, and he grabs my arm.

"In your essay, you talk about how dance made you feel. You don't have to give up the rush. In fact, you need that passion. It's the only thing that will get you through." He lays something in my hand—a brand new set of wide satin ribbons for pointe shoes that must have fallen out, too. "I want to spend time with you. However you'll let me."

"Because I'm your type?" I murmur. "I get that you make a habit of crossing lines. But there are some I can't live with."

"Why is that, Olivia?" Sawyer's staring at me with

the kind of intensity that burns a hole in my chest. His frustration is a living thing. "Are you afraid it says something about me or about you?"

Because the idea of him seeing another woman my age, of wanting her, of risking everything to be with her, hurts like hell. I want to believe what we have—had—was different.

But he never promised me that. It was only ever supposed to be hot, wild, a fantasy come to life. Maybe part of growing up is realizing when you're expecting too much.

"You're right," I admit.

"A first, where you're concerned." He looks around at the hall. "You have to teach another class?"

"I'm done." A notification beeps on my phone. "But I have to change and run an errand, then head home. It's Hoes Over Brews tonight."

His brows lift. "Excuse me?"

"Girls' night," I explain. "We talk about every-thing, including how dumb guys are."

"Well, I'm glad to provide you sufficient material for this evening."

The laugh bubbles up before I can stop it, and his eyes crinkle at the corners.

His apology can't undo the hurt, but it helps.

He returned my necklace, but didn't use that against me. He wasn't even going to take credit for it, which is so at odds with the man I met at the beginning of the semester—the one who'd use anything to get what he wants.

I fist the pendant in my hand. "Tell me how you got it back."

"Never."

"I could make you."

"There's nothing you could do to pry that information from me." I open my mouth. "At least not public," he amends with a grin.

Now that we're having an honest conversation for the first time in weeks, I don't want it to end. "I told the girls I'd pick up some things at CVS. You could come with me?"

There's nothing weird about running into my professor at the pharmacy, is there?

9

OLIVIA

"My roommate wants lube," I inform Sawyer as I grab a basket and head down the aisle. The section with condoms and other accessories appears, and I stop in front of it.

He turns the other way, inspecting the contents of the other side of the aisle. The wraps and bandages have me swallowing a laugh.

"You need sports medicine tape, Professor Redmond? I guess bone density decreases with age—"

"I'll tie you up with this, including covering your smart mouth."

Heat shoots straight down my spine.

It's not awkward to be here with him. Not at all.

Not that we used lube the one time we were together.

Really didn't need that.

But it could be fun…

Focus.

I'm scanning the brands when his voice interrupts me.

"Tell me about your toys."

Being back-to-back might feel safer, but it's an illusion. I can feel his heat from here, sense the mere inches between us even through my clothes.

"I have a vibe"—which he knows, because he made me use it—"but hardly a collection."

"Have you ever used it with another person?"

My fingers slip on the package I pick up. "No. But I like the idea of a bullet, like one of those clit vibes." My voice seems to have lowered an octave.

Sawyer turns to my side of the aisle and picks out a box of condoms. He drops it in my basket and I gawk at him.

"Presumptuous much?"

His eyes darken as he moves to stand in front of me, his body pressed against mine. He reaches into his wallet and pulls out a twenty, setting it on top of the box. "If you're using toys with someone, it better be me."

My heart hammers against my ribs as I glance up to see the mirror reflecting us from above.

He's tall, intimidating with his dark hair wild around his face. A decade older.

I'm smaller, but I look bold, too.

We look good together. Right and wrong in fascinating ways.

As we step away from each other, he says, "What else do you need?"

"Chips. Definitely chips."

He leads the way to the aisle.

"Pringles?"

"Hell no." I shudder. "We broke a bunch of cans working on the robot. If I never see another Pringles can again, it'll be too soon."

He chuckles while I pick out some Lays and add them to my basket.

"We need to talk about the other day in the supply room," I start.

"You were dripping on my fingers." I nearly drop the basket at the heat in his voice. "But the next time we play like that—"

"We weren't doing anything. You were being a massive prick."

"The next time we play like that," he repeats, "you'll be on board."

More chips are needed.

"You a chips or pretzels guy?" I ask as I toss

another bag in the basket so I don't combust from looking at him. Hell, one more.

"Chips. Pretzels don't have enough flavor per square inch."

"You would say that. No matter that pretzels are uniquely shaped and interesting."

"How are they interesting? They're all the same."

I laugh as I reach for Band-Aids.

"For?" he asks.

"I pulled out my pointe shoes the other day. Haven't had a chance to use the studio after classes are over, but soon, I'll find time."

"I'd like to see you dance. Watching you tonight turned me on like crazy."

A shiver runs through me at the thought of him across the room, unable to move or touch, aroused by the simple sight of me.

The idea of seducing him on purpose is insanely sexy. I've never seduced a man before. Sure, I've gotten dressed with a mind to how I'll look, but that's different than putting all of myself into making him think about, long for, beg for me.

He makes me feel things I've never felt, makes me brave and bold, reckless and free. The pleasure he brings me is more than I ever expected to experience—and we've only been together once.

I can barely imagine what else he could show me the next time—

"Professor Redmond."

It's a student, and I duck away to the cash register while he talks.

I sneak a look back over my shoulder as I pay.

But the way he hurt me comes back.

Think you can move on from him when he finishes this class and leaves?

I've dated Adam. Stuck with him long after I wanted to and had to get out.

This is different.

I'm different.

He walks me back to the parking lot outside the dance studio. Every step, I'm aware of him. I feel alive.

When we stop beside my car, he clears his throat. "I need to ask you something. It's awkward."

I laugh. "You talked about spanking me and bought me condoms. What could be more awkward?"

"The fish. The black one seems to be shedding. Something's wrong." A frown. "I've been feeding it, all of them, and I did some research..."

I barely hear what he says next because there's so much pressure in my chest.

Sawyer, who didn't give a shit about the fish, is

worried about them. And he's embarrassed and frustrated he needs to ask for help.

"That one is sensitive. Could be fungus. They can contract it in the wild, but it's more common with pets." My chest tightens in compassion. The poor animal did nothing wrong, but he's suffering.

I pull up a page on my phone. "Check all the water levels. Twice. Then get this antibacterial stuff and use it as directed."

"If it doesn't help?"

It's dusk and the sun leaves streaks of orange on the horizon, but it's nearly dark.

"If it doesn't...you know where to find me." I smile but he only sighs.

"Olivia. I like what we had. I want it back," he says.

The determination on his face is beyond sexy.

I want that too.

Both because of how alive he makes me feel, and because he's glorious. A dark god who casually brings mortals to their knees, benevolent enough to make sure they delight in their submission.

And I'm past judging myself for that.

But I think of how much it hurt to learn I wasn't the first younger woman he pursued. If I hadn't gotten so caught up in who he was as a person, it wouldn't have mattered nearly as much.

"Fine." I can indulge in the hedonism that is Sawyer Redmond, and protect my heart. "But it's only physical."

He frowns. "I'm not going to stop looking out for you. I care what you're doing, and with whom."

I think of the necklace, and the way he showed up in lab.

"We're not going on dates. Or playing games. Or hanging out. And that's not up for negotiation."

Which is exactly what this is when he steps closer and pops the collar on my jacket, his thumb grazing my neck. "We're exclusive. No other man touches you."

My heart skips under his touch. "And you don't touch any other women."

"Obviously." Sawyer stares at me like I'm insane, except it's not obvious to me, and hearing him say that has a knot loosening in my chest.

"Deal. But we're not texting."

He holds open my car door with a look of incredulity.

"You deleted our messages," I remind him. "If we're going to do this, we need to trust each other."

He grimaces. "You think that's why I deleted the messages."

"Why else?"

He holds out his phone and shows me the messages on his phone—perfectly intact.

I scroll through them, trying not to get emotional.

He owns a piece of our history I don't have anymore.

Does he read them? The thought makes my pulse skip.

"Delete them," I say.

His eyes narrow to slits. "What?"

"If I don't have our texts, you don't either."

He turns it over, long enough for a group of teenagers to wander past the parking long and cackle over some joke. Longer than I've ever seen him think on anything.

Finally, he says, "I'll send them to you."

"Fine." I say it as if I don't care, when it feels like I've suddenly been granted another chance at life.

He holds out a hand for his phone. "Need yours too."

I pass it over.

He hits a few keystrokes on mine, then returns it before typing into his. "There. Don't let some asshole take them from you this time."

I shove my phone in my pocket and set the bags in the passenger seat before I shift into the car.

I turn and look up at him. "If we do this, I have two more conditions."

He looks pained. "You want me to hand you my balls, too? I promise this will be far less satisfying if I do."

My lips twitch. "First..." I take a steadying breath. "I'm taking the money he left me. All fifty thousand."

If my dad truly is broke, I'll need it for tuition next semester.

He nods. "It's yours. And the other condition?"

"You have to give your dad a chance."

"He's dead."

"That's why it matters even more. You're carrying around the memory of him, but what if he changed? You don't want to entertain the possibility of that?"

His eyes bore into mine. "You don't know what happened the night I left."

"Then tell me."

What was the thing that pushed Sawyer over the edge, had him running from the only home he knew, even if it was imperfect at best?

He leans in and his breath is on my lips, warm, sweet.

"Tell me," I repeat, whispering against his mouth.

"No feelings, right?" he counters.

Damn him.

My fingers tangle in his hair as he pushes me against the back of the seat and drives into my mouth.

His hands hold my hips in place, sliding down until his fingers touch the top of my thighs, and I break the kiss.

He bites my lip and releases it, looking at me with raw desire.

He's not gone five minutes before my phone buzzes.

The name on the contact makes me laugh.

Repentant Asshole: Text me tonight.

OLIVIA

Liv: You can get the fish medication at the PopTart.

Repentant Asshole: The what?

Liv: I mean PetSmart. Whoops. I've had three beers.

Repentant Asshole: Tipsy Cherry.

Liv: That's not a thing.

Repentant Asshole: It is and I like it :)

Liv: I'm having drinks with my roommates.

Repentant Asshole: Glad you've been thinking about me.

Liv: Barely.

Repentant Asshole: If I was there, I'd lift you up on the table and make you show me how wet you are.

Liv: Sawyer there's a room full of people.

Repentant Asshole: Then I'd put that slickness to good use and teach you what it's for.

Liv: You wouldn't.

Repentant Asshole: Maybe, maybe not. But now you're gonna be thinking about it all night.

Repentant Asshole: See you in class, Cherry.

The email asking for me to stop by the dean's office comes the next afternoon.

"What's it about?" I ask Betty when I head upstairs.

"No idea," she says, frowning.

I have no desire to see him, but I can't very well ignore the summons.

The dean calls me in. "Olivia, good to see you."

He motions for me to take a seat in one of the leather chairs opposite him.

I sink into the chair but my attention is drawn to the walls boasting photos of graduating classes.

"Where's Professor Redmond's class? It's not up there."

"Must be a mistake."

"Wait, here it is." I find it out of order, at the far

end of the others. Sawyer's in the picture, gorgeous but also somber, his dark eyes haunted.

"I don't think you should get attached to Professor Redmond. He won't be here long."

I shift in my seat. "Because he's covering Lancaster's class only until you can replace him and he can go back to New York?"

"He'll be going somewhere, but it won't be New York." As if remembering himself, his composure returns. "The department is questioning its investment in the Stars competition."

My gaze snaps to his, the photos forgotten. "But we just qualified through regionals."

"I appreciate that. But it was one of Lancaster's particular interests. He had a long history with the department and was allowed certain indulgences. Now that he's passed, we need to re-prioritize."

I remember reading that the department's budget has been cut relative to the business school and the law school. I guess even at a well-funded school, some areas get relatively less attention.

"Have you talked with Professor Redmond about this?"

"It's not his decision. It's mine."

No.

The team is finally getting along. We have a real chance. I won't let this end.

It means everything to Royce and Madison and me. Just as much as for us, I want this for Sawyer. This matters to him.

My mind spins. I'm not good at playing games, but now, I need to be.

"But before regionals, you said there were companies interested in our work?"

"Interest is a long way from dollars."

I take in the photos on the other side of the room. They're still formal, but contain only a handful of people and feature ribbon cutting ceremonies, awards, and men in suits with big checks.

That's what speaks to the dean.

I think of the voicemail sitting on my phone from the attorney about the money Lancaster left me. He would want this to succeed—for me, and my class-mates, and for Sawyer.

What about tuition? There's a real chance my family won't help.

If the project gets shut down, Royce is screwed. Everything we work for flies out the window.

Now, not a few months from now.

"My father has been difficult for you to get hold of. But he's excited about this project. And has been meaning to support it."

The dean shifts forward, steepling his hands. "Is that so?"

"Would fifty thousand be enough to signal his commitment and keep the project on track?"

The dean blinks, gesturing with a hand. "Of course, that would be a welcome contribution."

I stand, my heart racing.

"Good. Then I suspect you'll be getting a check soon."

"Shit, shit, shit," I mutter as I drop into a seat in the corner of the library foyer and open my laptop.

Preparatory call: Northeast Stars competition teams.

When I open my web browser, the banner announcing the call takes up most of the screen.

I'm regretting telling Royce and Madison I had it under control. It's midterms and everyone's busy. Which is why I'm late—after a beaker exploded in my chem lab, I ran late cleaning it up and going through hazardous material protocols. I bolted to the first location I could find to take this call.

I pull up my Notes app on the side of my screen before entering the passcode into the browser window.

No luck.

The clock says the meeting started three minutes ago. Maybe they're running even later?

I try another code and it sends me through.

Finally.

But only one other face pops up on the video screen.

"What are you doing here?" a woman with dark braids pulled back in a headband demands.

"I'm here for the Stars competition call."

"Me too. But we're in the wrong room. Aliya," she volunteers.

"Liv."

She screws up her face and I hear the clack of keyboard keys. From her smooth skin, she can't be more than a few years older than me.

"What are you doing?"

"Trying to hack into the feed."

That kind of computing is way beyond me. Royce could probably do it, but he's not here.

I catch sight of something over her shoulder, suspended from the ceiling in what I'm guessing is her room. "What is that?"

"A hang glider I made…"

"Wow."

"…in eighth grade."

Damn. She's super smart.

"Aerodynamics is my first love," she says breezily.

"When I was vice president of the engineering society at our school, we brought in an entirely new course on it."

"So you've graduated."

"Yup. I'm involved in the Stars program peripherally—as an alum advisor for people who need help."

"You competed when you were in school? How did it go?"

"We won. I got funding for my company."

I'm a little awestruck. "What's that like?"

"Intense. It's not like school, where everything comes down to what's technically possible. It's a big world and so much more matters. But you can also be a bigger piece of the puzzle—work on longer term projects, if you have the funding."

I click back into the calendar invitation and send off a message to the organizer saying we can't get in.

No response.

"Do you know what the new requirements are?" I ask, tapping my pencil against the paper.

"Hmm?"

"I mean, that's the point of being on the call." I surf around websites to see who won last year. "It looks like they had press releases about a new lead sponsor this year. Which could mean the companies don't have money to sponsor or it's less appealing."

She laughs. "Nice observation. When I did the

competition, there wasn't even a phase where you submitted a statement of purpose. You could stick one throwaway line in your presentation about the applications of your work and be done with it."

"Bingo." I notice the same thing online. "That's what they're trying to do. They want projects that are exciting. But"—I chew my lip—"we have less than a semester to make it perfect."

"It doesn't need to be wrapped up in a neat little bow. In fact, better if it's not. Gives you time to build something awesome after."

I think about the applications we've discussed as a team.

"Know what would be cool? Helping to preserve the world we have." I repeat some research about underwater ecosystems that I found while looking up caring for Lancaster's fish as Aliya keeps typing away.

My email dings and there's an apology from the organizer with a PDF document summarizing the changes.

"What's your email address?" I ask Aliya.

She tells me.

"Incoming." I forward the document.

"Thanks. Hey, I'm running an online roundtable for prospective engineering students in high school in a few weeks. We had a speaker back out. You should join."

"Me? But I'm not even an engineer yet."

She cocks her head, sending dozens of tiny braids cascading over one shoulder. "You think about how to save the world, I'd say you're a pretty good one."

12

OLIVIA

Liv: How're the fish?

Repentant Asshole: Look for yourself. Here's a picture.

Liv: Much better.

Repentant Asshole: It's hot that you know how to heal living things.

Liv: Are you trying to get in my pants, Professor?

Repentant Asshole: Mm-hmm. Holding fish hostage is the number one way to lure a woman into bed.

.   .   .

e're back on.

The long looks.

The hot texts.

The simmering awareness under my skin that makes me feel like I'm living a life beneath a life.

School and friends can't possibly compare with the reality that is Sawyer Redmond's attention.

The difference is I'm smarter this time. We're doing it on my terms.

Okay, *our* terms.

No feelings for me.

Exclusive for him.

All weekend, we text.

We still haven't found a moment since that hot kiss by my car outside the studio, because I've thrown myself into work after talking with Aliya and agreeing to sit on her panel.

Monday in class, I wear the tightest jeans I own, a thin sweater that hugs every curve, and black heeled boots.

When I join a group of students getting his signature on some documents for the team, he slips a sheet of paper on top of the signed form.

.   .   .

You're trying to make me hard.

I flip it over and write back.

Glad it's working.

I return to my seat and my phone vibrates.

Repentant Asshole: Meet me in the supply room of the design lab.

Liv: My ass still hurts from the last time.

Repentant Asshole: Bet you're still wet from it, too.

He's on me the second I arrive, dragging me against his very hard, very aroused body.

"You wore this for my benefit?"

"You like it?"

"Love it." His eyes darken with desire as he closes the door and turns me to face it.

My cheek hits the side but my gaze skims down the aisles. "I've been thinking about this project. What if this robot isn't only inspired by nature? What if its purpose is to help nature?"

He stares back at me.

"There are robots used in diving for all kinds of purposes like off-shore drilling, or patrolling ships to look for contraband. But I was doing some research about environmental remediation—"

"You want to save the fish," he finishes.

"Yeah, Sawyer. I want to save the fish."

"What are you looking for?"

"A big glass box. Something we can fill with water. If the robot is going to function in an aquatic environment, it has to float."

"You're crazy."

I roll my eyes. "It's not doable?"

"You didn't design with those specs in mind. You'll need to change metals, and have some kind of—"

"Ballast system to control how it goes up and down," I finish. "The judges want something that's important. Saving the oceans is important."

He shakes his head and starts down the aisle.

He's almost down the other end of the row.

Seriously? My idea is so terrible I'm not even getting laid anymore?

He leans into the shelving, finding a sheet of glass.

He's helping.

My chest expands.

He slides the sheet out and lays it against the shelves.

"Thank you," I say and mean it.

The next second he's got me backed against the shelves. The expression on his face is lust, but more than that. "You're welcome."

He takes a breath. "Did you enjoy it when I spanked you?"

The hard right should be a relief, but it's not. "Yes. And no."

"Because you were afraid."

"Because I wondered whether you did it with her, too."

He turns away. "I barely knew her, and she's practically a kid."

"And I'm not."

"No. You're not." He closes the distance between us and my heart stops. "You're a woman. A challenge. An escape from a life I thought was destined to be filled with predictable, judgmental people."

The cold metal shelving presses against my shoulders but all I feel is the warmth of his gaze.

I look down and see him slide his fingers down my jeans, inch by inch. "What kind of lesson is this?"

"A reminder. When two things collide, both are changed by it."

I don't have time to ask him what he means because a finger rubs across my clit.

The ribbons of pleasure make me gasp, my nipples pulling tight beneath my bra.

"Fuck. You this ready for me all the time, sweetheart?" His voice is a drug.

He doesn't stop there but presses inside me. Pleasure spikes through me and I squirm, to get closer or farther away, I'm not sure.

Before I can decide, a second finger joins the first, stretching me.

The heel of his hand holds me there, grinding against my clit, but it's his eyes that pin me in place.

I grab the shelf behind me and brace myself as his fingers rub my clit in fast circles.

"Yes. Harder." My voice is thick with sex, because I'm already so turned on. I reach with trembling hands to unfasten my jeans and shove them down my legs, giving him better access.

He groans his approval, sliding a third finger inside me, and I don't know how I stand.

"This better than the last time you were in lab?" he teases.

"My fingers are still scratched from building circuits and my ass was sore for two days."

The bulge behind his fly twitches.

"Did that seriously turn you on?" I manage.

"We've established I'm a twisted man, Cherry."

He might call this a lesson, but it's not. Nor is it a punishment like the last time we were in here.

This is a reunion. A reminder of what we create together.

"I'm going to come," I gasp.

"Not yet." He easily pulls my hips out, hitching my leg around his waist. "Want to feel you when you do. It's been too long."

He unzips his pants and takes out his cock. I forgot how big he was, how thick and hard.

I fish in my bag for the box of condoms from the CVS. I take one out and start to rip open the package, but he takes it before I can.

His lips brush my fingertips, the skin that's still sore from all the work in the lab.

"I got it."

It's a fucked-up kind of sweet when Sawyer rolls the condom on and positions himself between my thighs.

But all sweetness evaporates the moment he grabs my hip and thrusts inside me.

He's so wide it's hard to take, but he doesn't stop until he's all the way in.

"So tight." His voice is hot praise. Whatever we're doing, I can't help feeling like I'm getting an A.

A big one.

He starts stroking into me, finding an angle that's better than anything I've found myself.

All I can think about is the building pressure to come, and his driving forces me to the edge.

His hand grabs my shoulder and the other takes my hip. He pulls me back onto him. His free hand slides down my belly, touching my clit.

"I'm going to watch you come," he says, his voice so deep it shakes me. "If you're good, I'll make you come again."

I'm having a hard time even standing with all the pressure and it's not helping that his cock is hitting me in just the right spot.

He increases the pressure and speed on my clit and I shudder. Heat spreads across my skin.

"Cherry, I was wrong. You're fucking perfect."

I hear the distinct rhythm in his voice that says he's close to coming, and I work myself to the same tempo.

I'm going to come. I'm going to come. I'm going to come.

Then I'm breaking, pleasure detonating deep inside me and rippling outward.

His hand connects with my ass and the shock has every muscle clenching.

"Again."

When he re-enters from behind, I'm a goner.

He drives harder.

I explode as I scream his name and fall forward against the shelf, my leg slipping as I shift.

And I kick the sheet of glass.

There's a shattering sound behind us.

"Oh my God. I..."

But he doesn't stop.

A shudder runs through him and he pushes hard a final time and holds me as he finishes.

"Shit!" Reality sinks in as I realize I destroyed the pane of glass we were going to use. "I'm the worst team lead ever."

Sawyer chuckles. "We can order more glass."

His face is close. I want to kiss him.

"We have lots of lessons to make up, Cherry. I'm going to have you on the desk." He deepens his voice. "I'm going to have you on the floor." He nibbles my neck, kissing up and down the side. "I'm going to have you against the door."

My eyes squeeze shut. I told Madison this was over. I swore I'd put the team first.

As I straighten my clothes, I realize they're not the only issue. "What's the dean's problem with you?"

Sawyer adjusts his cuffs. "He lied on an important paper five years ago. It stopped him from getting tenure."

"How is this your fault?"

"I was his research assistant who worked on the paper."

I can't wrap my head around it, Sawyer working with—for—the dean.

"There was an investigation. He was never formally disciplined, but the cloud of it hung over his head. He wanted to get in closer with my father. For all his flaws, he was influential, with an impeccable academic record."

"Until this."

He nods.

"He went and taught at another school before coming back. I'm not sure how he brokered this deal."

I turn that over. There's still a piece that doesn't click. "Why do you care that the dean wanted to get in close with your father? Your dad was a dick to you."

"He made sure I had good grades and opportunities."

"Oh, so he wasn't all evil," I prod, and am rewarded by a dark look.

Sawyer cups my ass, pulling me against him. "Whatever redemption kick you're on, it's not gonna happen."

"Because you think your relationship with your dad isn't worth saving?"

"You'd give anyone a second chance."

My arms loop around his neck. "And aren't you glad I did?"

I tug at my lip, but Sawyer captures my finger and presses it to his own. I brush softly over the bow of his lip, and suddenly he sucks my finger between his teeth.

This is so good.

He's so good.

I can't believe we're doing this again. My body is still shaking from what just happened, and already, I'm greedily plotting ways to have more.

"There are things we can't do in the supply room," he murmurs after releasing me. "We could go to a hotel."

"Or your place."

"There's not much to see. The porch is still off.

I'm going to finish it in the next few days so the realtor can get working on it again."

I start down the aisle away from him. "Send me a picture."

"Of my realtor?"

"No!" Thinking of the woman draped over Sawyer at Fall Ball has dark jealousy rising up. "Of the porch. Preferably of you working on the porch. Shirt optional."

"Or I could send you a picture of my cock when I'm thinking of you late at night." His grin is delicious, and my throat dries.

"That works too."

"Tell you what. Next Thursday night, I'll find us a place. You're mine all night long. You need to catch up on my lessons."

"It's midterms, Professor. Girl's got to study."

"I'll drill you."

I cock my head. "On my flashcards?"

"Anywhere you want, Cherry."

13

OLIVIA

The rest of the week and part of the next one are focused on classes and hooking up with Sawyer in between.

That doesn't stop us from arguing in class, or by text, or on the phone.

We hooked up in his office, in a closet in the university center after lunch, and even after dark behind the library Tuesday night.

It's reckless and addictive, and always over too soon because the threat of being caught is never far away.

A couple of times I scan R.U. Down with my friends, though I'm only halfheartedly interested in other people's gossip.

I have my own again.

Wanting Sawyer is the easy part. I'm a grown

woman and he's sexy and amazing and makes me feel things I thought weren't real.

He's also been warmer and more attentive with the team lately, and more generous with his time. The input he's given has come more like suggestions than commands.

I presented the idea of the diving robot to the team. Strangely, Madison was the first to get on board. She can convince Royce—he looks at her like she makes the sun rise over Campus Hill every morning.

Adam might take some work.

But when I explained underwater robots are helping in more lucrative applications too, like shipping and oil drilling, that seemed to placate him for now.

We have momentum for the first time. I'm starting to believe we can put forward an amazing project. Maybe even a winning one. The email that came through yesterday from the dean was the final act of what I put in motion last week.

Dear Olivia,

We received the check. Please thank your father.

. . .

The Dean

I pledged that money because I wanted to keep the Stars competition going. If it accomplishes that, it'll be worth it.

When I received the money from Lancaster's lawyer, the woman informed me he had intended to leave me a few other items but couldn't find a record of them. My curiosity was piqued but I told her it was fine.

Maybe Sawyer has a record of them, but I don't want to raise it right now. Not when things are good with us.

Tonight, on the way home from the studio after dance class, I call my mom.

"Hello?" Her voice comes through on the hands-free from my car a few blocks from campus.

"Hi, it's me. I wanted to check on some mail from school. Has my tuition bill for next semester arrived?"

"No, but your father's business assets are frozen."

My hands tighten on the steering wheel and I try to focus on the road. "What does that mean?"

"There's a full investigation into all of his spending, and we can't pay for anything new."

The streets pass in a blur as I navigate the final few corners and turn into the lot for my residence building.

I throw the car in park and stare out the windshield, my mind spinning. "He screwed up, didn't he?"

"We don't know that."

"Then someone else did. Why would they be investigating?"

"If they contact you, don't admit to anything," she hisses.

"Why would they contact me?" I struggle to keep up. "Wait. You said no new expenses, but there's still money for tuition next semester, right?"

"What about your family? Typical you'd think about yourself."

She clicks off and I stare out the windshield. What if the worst happens and we're left with nothing?

You had fifty thousand dollars, and you gave it away.

I head up to my room, legs heavy and face numb. Then I drop onto my bed, balling up a pillow and screaming into it.

Normally, I'd keep my frustrations about family to myself. But lately, I've turned to Sawyer.

He's been oddly respectful of our agreement to keep things physical. Enough that I have to remind myself once or twice that this time will be different. This time, I refuse to lose my heart.

Going to him is not the same as feelings. It's just...openness. He listens in a way that's strangely nonjudgmental.

I reach for my phone.

Liv: You around?

I chew my lip until dots appear.

Repentant Asshole: I finished the porch.

There's a picture of it, and it looks great. More than that, it's the first he's mentioned something other than our relationship or the fish since we got back to our arrangement.

Liv: Way to go, handyman. You were going to show me your tools.

. . .

Repentant Asshole: I had no idea you were so insatiable ;)

The next picture is of him, his zipper half undone and I can see the outline of his cock through the fabric.

Repentant Asshole: Going to shower. Talk soon.

He's the whole package—smart, gorgeous, competent. I want what's under his skin, not just what's under his clothes.

I know we can't, but that only makes me want it more.

SAWYER

"Dayum. It's finished," Daniel calls when he comes to my house early in the morning for our run. "You did a good job, too. You work hard enough, you could be a contractor someday. Maybe even an engineer."

I shove him and he dances out of reach with a grin.

"I'm more than an engineer. I'm a fucking cofounder of a company."

"Because you're in such a hurry to get out of here." He looks around. "This place isn't so bad, Sawyer. Must be something you like here."

I think of Liv. "Only one thing."

Since I ambushed her at the dance studio with an apology, we've negotiated a new deal. We're exclusive...which means her under me and only me.

Every time, it blows my mind. She blows my mind.

We're back to regular texting—flirting, teasing, and talking about her new Stars project ideas.

I want more.

Olivia can't stop me from caring about her, but we agreed to keep the feelings in check.

More like she decided to keep her feelings in check.

I've never gotten so attached to a woman before, never much cared what we called it. But where it used to feel wrong to be with her, now, it feels wrong to get into bed alone.

"You'll learn to appreciate simple life after you

have kids." Daniel's words bring me back. "Dropped Andy at daycare, he's singing my ear off. He's into music."

"Sounds like one of many reasons not to have them."

We hit the pavement, the thud of our footfalls and the slow burning in my lungs familiar. "My dad had a collection of knickknacks, including a couple of drums. You wanna take a look? Maybe Andy wants some."

"The 'my ears are already bleeding' part of me says no. But the 'good dad' part of me says yes."

We do a loop through campus and back, enough to make me feel alive.

When we return, he follows me inside and takes a look. "You don't want to keep any of this for yourself?"

"Nah. I don't need memories of him."

But my gaze runs around the room, landing on a telescope in the corner.

The store was full of pieces and gadgets, each one fascinating my young eyes.

"You earn the right to explore out there by understanding what's on Earth."

"But what if learning about what's out there can teach us about Earth?" I countered with an eleven-year-old's logic.

He stared me down, a hint of admiration in his stern face, but he wouldn't bite. So I built one myself with mirrors and parts from around the house.

The magnification was limited. When he saw how hard I worked, he got me the real thing.

It was the only time I can remember him getting me something I wanted.

Daniel takes a few things and after, I shower and dress for the day and feed the fish.

I hit a contact.

"Hey," I say when Olivia picks up the video call. I'm rewarded by her pretty face, hair slicked back like she's recently gotten out of the shower. "Check this out."

I flip the phone around to show her the fish. "He's almost back to normal."

"Hell yes! Behold, the fish whisperer!" Her muffled applause and catcalls make me snort.

"I'm a fish mercenary," I correct as I head out the door to the porch I'm actually pretty damned proud of. "I expect a reward."

"After I figure out how to sell my car."

"What? Why?" I pull up halfway down the walk.

"My dad's company is going down. I need to make tuition."

"But you have the money from my dad."

She hesitates and my grip on the phone tightens.

"You spent it already. On what?"

"School stuff." Her voice is distant, almost avoiding.

"Clothes? Rent?"

"I don't want to get into it."

She's younger, but this is a new reminder.

I try to rein in my temper as I take the steps down. She's not only my student, she's the woman I can't stop thinking about. One who's given me more than money can buy—her body, her trust, a fresh start.

I care about her, and I hate watching her struggle.

"I'll give you the money."

"No."

"Why not?" I demand, shifting into the Mercedes.

"Because I'm sleeping with you."

"What're you gonna do? Dance at Velvet for everyone in this damned town?"

"I'll get a loan."

"Or you could take the money from me."

"When was the last time you lent some woman you were sleeping with twenty grand?"

I lean back against the head rest, sighing. "It's not a loan. It's a gift. And you're not some random woman. We're exclusive."

"Just because I have complete unfettered access to your dick..."

The laugh catches me off guard. "Unfettered? Nice."

"...doesn't mean you give me thousands of dollars."

It's a reminder that I'm not supposed to care about her.

When the fuck did I start following anyone's rules but my own? When did I ever try so hard?

Since she made us conditional on keeping feelings out of it.

She gets under my skin, and every time I see her, I get closer to losing my whole damn heart.

"Well, if you could take care of yourself, it wouldn't be a problem. But you can't." The words are out before I can stop them.

The endless seconds of silence are confirmation something has gone horribly wrong.

"I have to go."

"Come on. Olivia. I didn't mean—"

She hangs up and I rub a hand over my face.

Don't need a damned PhD to know I'm going to regret that.

14

———

OLIVIA

"Nice bra." Kat nods to my shoulder and I glance down to see the inch of black lace strap exposed by my wide-necked shirt. "How long have you guys been back on?"

"A few days." I ignore the salad on my plate and the bustling lunch traffic of the University Center, lowering my voice. "It's not a relationship. I mean, it is, but it's only sex."

They exchange a look and Kat reaches for her glasses. "So what's the problem? Besides the fact he might as well be your vampire lover because you can't ever be together in the light of day."

Yesterday on the phone, he tried to help me—but he also implied I couldn't take care of myself.

"I don't want him to think of me like a student."

"But you are a student. And he likes you the way you are."

"Well, maybe I don't like me the way I am."

"Which is?"

Helpless.

I took Lancaster's money, and I don't regret it. But now Sawyer's offering me his, and it feels terrible.

My phone buzzes with a text. A picture of the black ghost knife fish comes through.

Repentant Asshole: Captain Jack is hungry.

Liv: You named him? How do you know it's a male?

Repentant Asshole: Apparently the only definitive way to tell is during breeding, but there's a general consensus that females' eyes are closer to the front while males' are more on the sides.

Of course he looked it up. The image of him doing serious fish research pops into my head and tugs on my heart without permission.

I type back.

· · ·

Liv: Right. And why is he hungry?

Repentant Asshole: Because the asshole who usually feeds him has been distracted all day thinking about a woman who's angry with him.

Liv: I'm not angry. It sounded as if you think I'm a kid who can't take care of herself.

And that sucks way more than not having enough money to pay for school, I think but don't say.

Dots appear for a minute, then two.

Repentant Asshole: I know you can take care of yourself, but I wanted to look out for you. For most of my life, I didn't have control over my circumstances. So when I can do something for someone who deserves it, I will.

· · ·

Repentant Asshole: Plus I don't like seeing you hurt. It fucks me up.

Repentant Asshole: Are we still on for tonight?

My chest squeezes. Dammit. For a man who's good at getting into trouble, he's remarkably good at getting out of it too.

"What are you going to do, hold him down and insist you're a grown-ass woman until he agrees with you?"

Kat's words drag my attention back.

I adjust my shirt, tucking the bra strap away, and an idea takes shape in my brain.

"That's not the worst plan."

I head to Velvet with a bag full of gear.

The security guy out front is the same one who worked the night I came with the girls and met Sawyer for the first time.

His nod is full of recognition, and his gaze drops to my legs. "You gonna pull another move for me to let you in here?"

I grin. "Nope. Teresa said you have to let me in."

Inside, the place is empty, the sleek tables and couches around the perimeter, the glossy stage and pole. My stomach flips.

"When he gets here," I tell the guy, "have him sit here."

I head to the bar where a woman is stocking for the night. "Hey. Do you think you'll be done with that soon? I can help if you like."

"You really want this place to yourself, huh?" She pulls out a spray bottle of Lysol. "Just wipe down whatever you use when you're done."

It's probably a joke, but as I go backstage to get ready, I'm still not sure.

I take my time doing my hair and makeup, then pull on the costume I put together.

He's here.

I know the second before I hear him and the security guy talking on the other side of the stage.

"I don't want to sit. Where is she?"

I wait five seconds.

Ten.

There's no more arguing outside. I peer through the curtains, relieved the bar is vacant now.

When I texted earlier to tell Sawyer there was a change of plans and to meet me at Velvet instead of a hotel, he wanted to know what was going on. I didn't answer, just told him to be here.

Sure enough, there's a man sitting in a lone chair in front of the stage.

Adrenaline shoots through me.

When I locked eyes with Sawyer at Velvet that first time, it was so sexy.

I can only imagine how it'll feel tonight.

No audience.

No interruption.

No threat of discovery.

Just him and me and the way we talk best.

And I need to show him I'm not some girl who can't stand on her own two feet.

I start the music, a low throbbing beat.

When I step out onto the stage covered in shadows from the spotlights, the tables are empty— the place is mine—and I'm wearing a short dress with very little beneath it.

Sawyer's eyes are on me. "What are you doing?"

I'm supposed to be the one on display, but he's so beautiful it steals my breath. His rugged jaw flexing, dark hair spilling to his shoulders, intensity pouring off him.

I take a steadying breath. "Do you ever think about what it would've been like if we'd met under difference circumstances? Like maybe if we met in

New York instead of here? Or maybe you watched me dance at the ballet, instead of in a T-shirt and jean shorts?"

"I'm not good at make-believe, Cherry."

That's why I borrowed this place for tonight. I wanted to feel strong and feminine and capable.

The music is indescribably sexy.

The dance is one I've been working on in my head, some of my classical training and flexibility. I made it more provocative once I decided on my plan for tonight.

"I'm not a kid."

I take a slow step toward him, and his eyes burn down my body.

"I know that."

My feet stop out of reach of his chair. "You say you do, but you don't. If this is going to work, I need you to."

I peel the dress over my head. Underneath, I'm wearing a sheer black bra and thong. The bra has embroidered cherries over the nipples, and the thong has matching ones at the "T" in the back.

His eyes darken. "Olivia..."

A thrill races through me as I drop the fabric on the ground.

Velvet might not be the real world, but for tonight, it can be our world.

I shimmy in front of him, moving my hips slow and rhythmically.

When I lean in and lower the bra straps to my elbows, he starts breathing more heavily.

"Your tits are perfect."

"Only my tits?"

He grins. "The rest of you is okay, too."

I slide the bra down to my waist and his hungry gaze snaps down my body.

He leans forward, but I put the bra back in place. "No touching the dancers," I murmur against his mouth, pulling back teasingly.

"You're touching me."

My skin heats everywhere, and I go deeper into the fantasy. "One of us is going to be in trouble. Because I'm in an exclusive relationship."

"Relationship."

That's not what was supposed to come out.

"I meant arrangement."

No feelings.

My own demand.

But the lines are blurry.

"I hope he fucks you for this," he says, eyes wild, breath ragged. Then he takes my mouth in a kiss that's just as rough as his voice.

I sink into his lips, because he's the storm I want to lose myself in. I'd rather be swept away with this man than hide away in the safety of everything I know.

When he pulls back, I feel the hairs on my neck lift. I look past Sawyer toward the door.

"He's watching," I whisper. "The security guy."

My skin prickles and I have a sudden urge to reach for my dress, but it's halfway across the floor.

Sawyer's body goes tight. "How does it make you feel?"

It's like the audience the first night. Strangers' eyes, with strangers' minds behind them.

"I can end it in a second," he promises. "But tell me how it makes you feel."

I have no desire to be with another guy, to have him touch me, but feeling his gaze on me awakens an urge I've never experienced.

"Hot."

Sawyer's eyes darken. He looks past me toward the door. "Show's over. I catch you watching again, you won't be able to walk, not to mention work the door here or anywhere."

The door closes immediately.

"If you were going to do that, then why did you ask?"

"Because I wanted you to trust me enough to tell me the truth. To keep you safe. That's the greatest gift you could give me."

Warmth erupts inside me, but there's gooseflesh on my arms and neck. Every time I think I'm used to this raw, earnest man, he proves me wrong.

He circles my waist with his hands, palms warm and possessive on my bare skin.

I'm practically naked but I feel sheltered. Cared for. Seen.

"When was the last time you had a lap dance?" I breathe.

"If I've ever had one, I can't remember it."

"If you've ever had one, I'm going to erase it from your memory."

I try to shift off his lap but he won't let me.

"You don't have to prove anything to me, Olivia," he murmurs against my throat. "I see you. I want you. I care about you."

Every muscle in me goes lax.

"Not how you dress. Or how you act. Or how you dance. I see who you are when you think no one's paying attention. When you think the world is wrapped up in its own drama, and there's no hope for any of them... I'm watching you."

My heart seizes. I can't look in his eyes right now or I'm going to lose it.

So instead I arch my back and rub against him.

He feels so good and eager and I think of how it

would feel to have him inside me when the music reaches a crescendo.

He leans forward, grabbing my bra strap between his teeth and snapping it against my skin. "Take it off."

"You want to add that to your collection, Professor?"

His eyes are hooded, hazy with lust as I reach back to unhook my bra one-handed.

I can hear his breath catch as my bra comes undone and I lower the straps.

I rub against him as I dance before him, getting myself off. I'm high on my power and the sex between us. It overwhelms me and he senses it.

"Take off the rest," he says huskily.

"Be patient."

"We'll see who's patient when I suck on your clit until you're begging to come, sweetheart."

Then his hands are on me, dragging me down to sit on him.

I slide my arms around his shoulders and my legs around his waist. He props his hands on my thighs and I feel him groan against me.

"If I met you under difference circumstances, it wouldn't have changed anything."

"No?"

I hear Sawyer's zipper come down as he opens

his pants and pulls out his cock.

Fuck. He's hard and he's huge, and my throat dries looking at him in the dim lights.

"No," he goes on. "Because in that world or this one, I'd still make you mine."

Tonight, I wanted to prove I'm the kind of woman who can take care of herself.

He obliterated any need to.

I wanted a moment of reprieve from the stress of campus.

He showed me it's not the minutes we have that matter, but how earnestly and unapologetically we use them.

I feel wild and free. Different from the girl who took the stage here months ago.

I skim my hands up my sides, lingering on my breasts in a way that makes his jaw work before threading up into my hair. "I want you to ride me until the sun comes up."

He reaches into his pocket for something, then rolls the condom over his cock.

My hips settle over him as his nose bumps mine. "Nothing in the world I'd like more, Miss Barclay."

It's not gentle—he's too worked up for that—but his hand grips my butt and he thrusts to meet me.

We're in a primal rhythm, me rocking on his cock, and I cry out.

He kisses me and I buck against him and he comes with me.

His beautiful body jerks under my hips and my hands and I feel powerful. Fearless.

The song is dying, the spotlights waning, but we're still joined and he's rubbing me while I tremble.

"Just a little more," he whispers in my ear.

I'm so wet, and when he moves inside me, I shudder.

As I come again, he grabs my hip and jerks me back onto him. His eyes are fierce with desire and something fiercer I don't dare name.

He drives into me all the way to the end. I grind against him, taking him deep enough it feels as if I couldn't separate us if I wanted to.

We're exhausted and we're sweaty and he's looking at me like he's never seen me before.

My eyes drift closed.

I feel exposed, but I also feel battered. Every part of me is bruised.

I'm not sure I can put all my pieces back together.

I'm not sure I want to.

"Olivia."

I blink to see him lean back in his chair, watching me like he's trying to memorize every feature.

"Come home with me."

15

SAWYER

She put rules on what this is.

Her body is mine.

Her heart, she keeps.

It's a lie.

Like she wanted, I ride her until she's exhausted. Then I let her sleep and wake her again in the early hours of the morning, make her come on my lips where I can still taste us both.

I wake to the sight of her already stirring next to me, her bare shoulder sticking above the white covers of my former bedroom.

It held a lot of bad memories, but I can't remember even one of them in this moment.

"How amazing is my hair?" she murmurs sleepily.

"Indescribable."

She starts to fix it and I pin her hands to the pillow, rolling over the top of her.

"You're perfect."

"A perfect mess."

I kiss her, because I can't do anything else.

Our relationship shifted last night.

I was already falling for her, but the way she looked at me...it wasn't only about her proving something.

All those promises my life would be better one day felt hollow until now. I spent my life trying to design and build something that would satisfy me, but never could.

Now I know why.

Because what I needed was flesh and blood.

"Tell me about your watch?" she asks as I start to fasten it on.

My fingers still on the leather band.

Whenever anyone's asked, I've said it was custom and let them wonder.

Now, my heart thuds in my ears.

"It's a piece of stone from the Brooklyn Bridge. It's where my mom...she died there." My chest tightens as I take in the lettering on the face. "It says, 'We choose.'"

Her cool hand on my cheek lifts my gaze and I stare at her earnest face.

"As a kid, I used to keep rocks from all over the place."

Shifting toward the edge of the bed, I reach into the nightstand of my childhood room and pull out a box.

When I lift the lid, she peers inside. Her lips curve. "Nice collection."

"They were something I could get when I was a foster kid. It didn't have extrinsic value. So I took one from every place I stayed."

From a garden or a shed or a corner. Unseen, undesired.

To me, they mattered.

She reaches into the box and takes a small pink stone, turning it in her fingers as if it's precious.

"You wanted a home. Some place you were loved and accepted for who you are. Is that why you want to give me the same thing?"

My chest cracks.

I want her to spend the entire weekend between these sheets, I want her to tell me all about the fish, I want to see if I can get an encore performance of that dance from last night that might ensure my cock stays in the upright and locked position for the rest of my life.

"I need to study," Olivia says against my lips

when she pulls away to get dressed. "Also, a gallon of coffee first because someone didn't let me sleep."

Evidently she had jeans and spare underwear in the gym bag—a shame, because I want to see her put on the fuck-hot dress she wore last night before stripping it off. But instead, she steps into skinny jeans and I have to satisfy myself with watching her curves as she wriggles into them.

"What're you doing?"

"The realtor's coming tomorrow and sent me a bunch of papers. I should at least look at them."

She pulls on a tank top, shooting me a glance over her shoulder that's way too knowing for a twenty-year-old. "The realtor returns."

I snort, grabbing clean briefs and tugging them on, followed by jeans. "It's her job. She's coming over to do...something with the house."

Olivia crosses to me, grabbing my jeans in one hand before I can fasten them. "I know exactly what she wants to do with 'the house,'" she breathes, making air quotes as her gaze runs up my body.

My grin comes easily. "You're cute when you're possessive, Miss Barclay."

I want the possessive, and more than that.

"Tell me something you haven't told anyone else," I say, impulsive, as I pin her against the window. It's a throwback to the night we met and the glint in her eyes says she knows.

Her attention skims over my shoulder, light dancing on her messily perfect hair. "Last night was the first time I've ever come in someone else's bed."

"In that case, it was also the second. And the third, if memory serves." My chest is warm, vibrating from the racing of my heart beneath my ribs. "You're serious."

"Yeah. That was a dumb thing to say." She tries to duck past me and hide her face, self-conscious, but I force her to look at me.

"It's not."

"Whatever. You've probably deflowered virgins in here."

This time she ducks under my arm, tripping toward the door and grabbing for a sweater in her bag.

"Guess it's my turn to tell you a secret," I call after her.

She pauses in the doorframe to pop her head through the neckhole of her sweater.

"I never slept with my partner's daughter. Never touched her. I've never been with anyone younger, before you."

She stills, her full lips parted. Shock blends with hope on her face. "You mean that."

I nod. It's all I can do with how she's looking at me. As if I'm holding the most precious gift out to her and asking if she wants it.

I didn't get why it meant so much to her, but right now, there's no question it does.

Remembering her task, she carefully pushes one arm through the sleeve, then the other.

"So she lied?"

"Her father pressured her. It was a ploy to push me out of my own company. I could've fought it harder, but she was an innocent caught in the cross-fires and it would've gotten ugly."

She tugs the sweater down her ribs, the smooth cashmere skimming over her figure. "Why didn't you tell me?"

"Because I wanted you to believe me first. Not to look at me with accusation, guilty until proven inno-cent." I reach for a shirt, shrugging into it for an excuse to avoid her eyes. "But perhaps at the same time, I didn't feel like I deserved your belief."

When I look back up, she's crossed the room to me.

Her arms wrap around herself, but her eyes convey the vulnerability her posture denies. "When she hit on you, you didn't even think about it? I don't blame you if you did."

My head shakes. "She was a kid."

"And what am I?"

The order to my chaos.

The face of my downfall.

The cause of my fucking heartbeat in my chest.

"A woman who's lived more than she pretends."

A flush crawls up her cheeks.

I can't help threading a hand in her hair as I draw her against me, all of her soft curves lining up with my hard edges.

We make out like teenagers.

Eventually, she pulls back. "We can't do this all day," she murmurs against my mouth.

"We absolutely can."

But she grins, and I readjust my cock in my jeans.

We pad downstairs, and the sound of two sets of footsteps has me happier than any noise has a right to make a man.

In the living room she trips on a box. "What's this?"

"Telescope. I was cleaning out his things."

She bends over the dark, smooth metal. "Then why does it have your name etched into it? In very awkward writing, I might add." Her lips twitch.

I groan. "It might have been mine. I can hardly remember."

"Where are these boxes going for the open house?"

I blink at her. "They don't have to go anywhere."

She looks around the living room at the stacks of boxes, sighing. "Tell you what. You make coffee, I'll start a list of what needs to be done." She reaches into her bag and pulls out a pink pen.

"What needs to be done is you have to study," I remind her. "I'll move these boxes after you go."

"And what will be left after that? How will you arrange things?" I meet her question with a blank stare. "Studying can wait a few hours. This is important."

"School is important."

"Sawyer, this place is a dump. Coffee." Olivia points to the kitchen.

My gaze narrows but I turn and start to do as she asks, my chest expanding for no good reason.

"We need something for the table in the foyer," she calls after me. "A focal point. Got anything for me?"

I'm not about to tell her it's cute how she takes charge. Cute and hot.

Like last night, she was sexy as hell. Watching her seduce me, I noticed her confidence rise with every sinful sway of her hips.

I enjoyed letting her have the upper hand.

It'll be that much more fun to go back the other way.

Daniel: You're joining me this afternoon at a house down the street.

Sawyer: For what?

Daniel: Integration into the local society.

Sawyer: We're too old to join a frat.

Daniel: If my sparkling conversation isn't enough, a few other faculty will be there.

It would take my mind off selling this house and my other issues.

I never invested much time in trying to make friends in a place because I was always leaving. But when Olivia texts to ask how the cleaning is going, I text back.

· · ·

Sawyer: All done. I'm going to someone else's house tonight.

Cherry: Better not be that realtor.

Sawyer: Hah. No, friends of Daniel's. Some guys have a kind of club.

The next second, my phone rings.

"What are you bringing?" Her breathy voice improves my mood immediately.

"Myself." I catch sight of myself in the mirror by the door. My hair's stuck to my face, there's dirt on my rolled-up shirtsleeves. "I might even shower and change."

"That's not enough."

"Wow. Way to cut a guy's ego."

Her laughter makes me smile, too. "Not what I meant. Bring food. Wine."

"Nope."

"Sawyer..." God, I love the way she says my name, like I'm a lost cause but she's not willing to give up anyway.

I head down the hall, taking in the work she

helped me do to tidy the space. On the kitchen counter, just visible from the hallway, there's a round pencil holder, with the pink pen she left here after making her list to help prioritize organizing.

But my favorite is the centerpiece on the foyer table: a dull metal bowl, full of apples.

"Why should I?" I tease, taking the stairs two at a time. "Because it's this unspoken rule? We've established I'm not much for rules."

"It has nothing to do with rules. It shows you care."

"It's transactional. I bring a fifty-dollar bottle so they let me in the door."

"It's not about the price. Bring a ten-dollar bottle if you like. Pick a label with a funny name. The intention matters as much as the execution."

"You're going to be a terrible engineer."

"Hey!"

"Kidding. It's like you and Daniel both want me to make friends here."

"Maybe I do."

Halfway to the top of the stairs, I stop. "Why is that?"

Because she doesn't want me to leave.

I've been getting those vibes from her, but dammit, I want her to say it.

She hesitates. "It helps having people on your side."

"You're on my side."

"Of course. But Daniel and I can't be the only ones. Making new friends is an important skill anywhere."

Right. My little do-gooder doesn't want me to be alone. It's not for any other reason.

"Just take wine," she pleads.

In my room, I yank the shirt over my head, the fabric sticking to my chest. "No promises."

I show up with wine.

Daniel's been a friend, because he knows my damage. Other people aren't nearly as cool with it. I'm not going to be friends with these people.

But when the door opens, the guy inside makes my brows rise.

He's tattooed. "New guy. And he brought wine. Cute. Come on in."

"Sawyer."

"Zander."

"You teach here?"

"Yeah. Literature." He sees me noticing all the

ink. "And yes, it was a fun job talk. All the old white guys stared a lot longer than you are."

I follow him down the hall. Inside the kitchen, Daniel's standing with another guy who introduces himself as Ricardo and explains he's in the fine arts department.

"Now before we start, you gotta swear a vow of secrecy about what's going down here tonight."

"You want a blood oath, you're asking the wrong guy. My palms are cut up enough from working on the house."

Zander tosses the wine in the fridge and pulls out a cold beer, holding it up. I shrug and he opens it, handing it over. Daniel and Ricardo already have them, and Zander takes another for himself and opens it.

"Mostly we keep it secret from Ric's wife."

"You're married."

Ricardo holds up a hand. "Happily."

"They're newlyweds. Wait until it wears off," Zander replies, and Ricardo throws a light punch at his shoulder that makes him wince, still grinning.

"That must have been from her. I know you can't hit like that."

We take our drinks into a TV room.

Zander drops onto one end of the couch. Ricardo takes a chair, and Daniel sinks onto the floor, extending his legs. I take the remaining spot on the couch.

I'm curious what they do here and don't have to wait too long to find out as Zander clicks on the remote.

The opening credits of a show filling the screen is vaguely familiar.

"Reality TV," I realize.

"Rival teams of treasure hunters travel the world and compete to find the biggest hauls," Ricardo confirms.

"We're highbrow by day, lowbrow by night," Daniel tosses over his shoulder.

"Your wife wouldn't let you watch it?" I ask.

"She'd let me but I'd never hear the end of it. Which is crazy because this is far more educational than Selling Sunset."

Ricardo grins and Zander smirks.

It's stupid and I like it.

"So they tried to take my office," Ricardo says at a commercial after Zander mutes the TV.

"Ricardo's getting the runaround on tenure," Daniel supplies. "Power struggles."

"This place isn't for me. The politics suck."

But Ricardo only grins.

"What?"

"It's a game. I told them I'd turn down a teaching load."

The easy way these guys deal with the bullshit makes me think about mine in a new way.

"But it's still garbage."

"So? You can make your own way without being bitter about it. And working anywhere else has the same problems."

"You don't get bored of assholes looking down on you?"

Zander smirks and spreads his arms—even the undersides are completely covered with color. "I like it when they look."

"Don't get attached," Daniel warns. "Sawyer's leaving."

"When?"

"End of the semester," Daniel looks at me to confirm.

I shrug, because the end of the semester suddenly feels too soon. "I have an open house tomorrow, but the property could take a while to sell."

"You want another drink?"

I said I'd come for one, but I'm in no hurry to leave.

"Yeah, I'll take another."

16

———

OLIVIA

The sociology text blurs together in front of my eyes.

I get up and flick on an extra light in the corner of my room. My roommates are out for the night—Kat at a party, Jules at a theater club thing.

Sawyer's a mile away, but it might as well be another world.

I'm rereading the underpinnings of capitalism so I can be in a position to graduate college in eighteen months while he's selling a house with his eager realtor at his side.

I'm grumpy, both because she's with him instead of me, and because I broke my own rules by playing house with him.

The way he opened up to me made it impossible to deny how much I care about him.

Earnest. I never expected this kind of earnestness from that man as when he told me about his ex-partner's daughter.

"I've never been with someone younger, before you."

He's raw and real, imperfect and irresistible. I want him, but more than that, I want to know he's mine and I'm his.

All I can think is how easy it felt to spend a morning with him. To talk on the phone over a simple question like meeting up with friends.

Telling him to make friends and bring wine...he probably thinks I'm crazy.

But what's even crazier is that I can't spend a day without obsessing over him.

Leaving his place to study was the hardest thing I've done in a long time.

I wanted to climb back into bed with him, to lose myself in the way he touches me and makes me feel like no one ever has.

I stare at my phone on the desk.

Through some miracle it rings. I reach for it, hoping it's Sawyer.

It's not.

"Mom. Everything okay?"

"Where are you?"

"At home, studying."

I reach for another text on my bookshelf—the

next one I'm going to hit up once I've finished prepping sociology.

"On the weekend?"

"Yeah. I've been slammed with lab work and I have a midterm coming up for my elective."

"Well. We need your car back."

The book thuds onto my desk as I release it. "What are you talking about? I paid for half of it with money from my internship last summer."

"Money from *his* company."

"But I earned it," I press. "I need it to pay for tuition."

This car is the only thing I have of value besides what's in my residence room.

"Don't take it out on me. The company is being investigated. All assets need to be accounted for." She pauses. "Your father wanted it back in forty-eight hours, but I told him you wouldn't have time given your school and social commitments. So do it by the end of the week."

I'm numb when she hangs up.

Our door buzzer sounds, and I hop up to answer. "Yeah?"

"Hurry up, babe, we're gonna be late."

"Adam?"

The next voice is even more surprising. "Let's go, fearless leader."

"Royce. What are you doing here?"

I buzz them up and a moment later, three people wearing black spill into my dorm.

"How come you're not dressed?" Madison chirps.

"For what?"

"The ultimate team challenge."

"Black Build. Don't tell me you forgot."

I blink. With all the stuff going on, I did.

Participating in the annual Engineering Society event, open to all engineering students of any year, never occurred to me. Last year, Adam and I did it but were nowhere near winning.

"But we have midterms. And after midterms, we have the justification to prep. This is a totally optional campus prank."

"We need to find all these items"—Royce holds up a list on his phone—"then make a tower in front of the engineering building."

Adam's grin disappears. "Basketball's been rough and you've been working your ass off to try to make this project work. I thought this would be a good chance for the team to, you know, bond. But if you don't want to hang out, we can go."

I stare into Adam's hopeful face.

This won't help us with Stars, but they want to do it. Me being with Sawyer has put pressure on our team. This could help.

"Okay. I'm in."

I go to my room and change into an all-black outfit of leggings and a long-sleeved turtleneck.

When I return, Royce's eyebrows lift. "Save the fish doesn't extend to save the cows?"

I glance down at my faux-leather leggings. "They're vegan."

"Oh, and we need your car," Madison says.

I hesitate only a moment before grabbing my keys and heading for the door.

On the way to the parking lot, we review the list together.

"Must be composed of no fewer and no more than twenty unique objects sourced from within a five-mile radius of Russell U," Royce rattles off. "Must be freestanding. Must be able to be disassembled after end of competition without use of torches or chemical agents. Bonus marks: items sourced from members of the campus community, not including the team."

"We could bust into the engineering building and try to get behind Betty's desk," Adam suggests.

Madison sighs. "What does she even keep there? I don't want to spend half our time breaking in if all we find are paperclips and coffee cups. That's not going to help us built an epic tower."

"She's right," Royce grunts as he rounds the back of my car.

"Wait. I've got this," I say as I shift into the driver's seat, thinking of his toolshed in the yard—it's got to have some tall, sturdy building materials. "We're going to Lancaster's house."

Madison narrows her eyes in the rearview mirror.

Adam switches on music, and Royce drums his fingers on the window in the back.

"What is this music?" Madison gripes, and Royce chuckles.

"What you'd rather have the holy trinity? Dolly, Reba, Shania?"

Her mouth drops open and I grin at her.

"You're a country fan?"

"Yeah, and I'm not apologizing for it."

I reach for the radio and flick it to a country station. "Before He Cheats" drifts lazily through my Bose speakers. "Carrie Underwood. Good enough?"

"Good enough."

I navigate the dozen blocks from campus, turning down Hot Profs Lane. I planned to park at the end of the street to avoid being seen, but now, I realize it's going to be out of necessity. Cars are lined up along both sides of the street.

This open house is bigger than I thought.

"How're we going in?" Adam asks after I park and we get out.

"We're not. I am."

I don't need them spotting Sawyer or tripping me up. I know this place.

Without waiting for agreement, I sneak up the driveway, using the parked cars as cover.

Even though my destination is the backyard, I can't resist leaning against the window to peek inside.

A dozen people make conversation. They're grown-ups, civilized.

When I spot Sawyer, my chest contracts.

He's beautiful in a dark shirt and dress pants, his hair loose and a half-empty glass in his hand.

The realtor's near him, all smiles and tossing him flirty looks.

I'm in stretchy pants and a beanie.

It's a cruel reminder of the reason I said no feelings in the first place. He's here to sell his house. He'll leave and go back to his life and I'll continue mine.

My attention drifts from Sawyer to an object in the corner of the room.

The telescope.

Scavenging from the backyard during a party is

risky but worthwhile. Breaking into the living room to take what's right under their noses?

It's insane.

But my mom's call drifts through my mind.

I'm tired of people telling me no, and Carrie's gotten under my skin singing about her baseball bat exploits.

I tiptoe around to the back door, using the key under the mat to get in.

No one's in the kitchen and I wait until the hall is clear to duck into the living room behind the couch.

The telescope's in the corner, where I suggested we set it for the open house.

I cross to it and grab it.

Then peek over the back of the couch at Sawyer, my breath catching.

He's so damn beautiful.

Get going. I creep back across the floor, my prize tucked under my arm.

I sneak a look behind me when I run into something.

Shit.

Apples spill out of the bowl and roll over the table. I grab for them, stopping them from rolling to the floor.

There isn't time to replace them all, so I stuff a couple back in and continue on my way.

I'm nearly out the front door when I'm thrown up against the wall in the hallway. The surprise makes me drop the telescope to the carpet.

Sawyer yanks the beanie off my head, recognition and surprise cutting the accusation on his beautiful face. "Well. Look who's stealing from me."

He's gorgeous and cultured, his dark blue shirt rolled down to cover the strength of his forearms, and pulling tight across his shoulders. His hair falls around his face, practically daring me to touch him. But it's the twist of his mouth that keeps me away.

"Borrowing. It's for Black Build."

"You broke into my father's home to take a telescope."

It sounds dumb when he says it like that. "I didn't break in. It is an open house."

"Didn't see you come in the front."

He's got me there.

"You miss me so much you couldn't stand to be away from me for twenty-four hours?" he asks softly.

Shit. He thinks I came to see him, that I'm being clingy.

"No. I came for Black Build. That's it." I cut a look toward the window. "My friends are outside."

His jaw works, like he's disappointed by my answer.

I reach for the telescope. "You had something I

needed. My team is waiting and I got what I need, so I'm going to go."

I start to duck out from between him and the wall.

Three steps down the carpeted hallway, his voice stops me.

"If you want to leave with that, there's a price."

My heart kicks in my throat as I turn.

"Don't move."

He stalks back into the living room, and my ears strain to hear him speak. There's nothing, only laughter and low music in the background.

A moment later, he's back.

He reaches for an apple on the table.

Then grabs my arm and yanks me up the stairs.

We leave the laughter and clinking wineglasses further behind with every step.

He releases me in the bedroom.

The room is dark, the rest of my team somewhere outside the window beyond.

Sawyer sets the apple on the bed, where it's illuminated by the sliver of light through the window.

"A room full of strangers are drinking sauvignon blanc twenty feet away. What are you going to do?" I breathe.

Sawyer reaches for his belt. "Remember how I said the next time we played you'd be onside?"

"Yeah."

"Tell me you're onside."

The arousal that's always there when I'm around him flares to life. How am I always less than three seconds from wanting to beg this man to fuck me?

I nod, eager.

He pulls out his cock and fists his hand in my hair, shoving me to my knees.

The door is wide open, the sounds of music drifting up the stairs.

"Anyone could come upstairs." Between the shock and getting the wind knocked out of me, catching my breath is near impossible.

"Then you'd better work fast."

I rock back on my heels, my boots digging into my ass as I look up at him from the carpet.

If I thought he was in command at the front of the class, he's even more commanding here. He's a dark god, thrilling and a little terrifying.

"Suck."

I tense, thinking of my team waiting outside. But this is the only way to get back out there with my prize.

He's as thick and hard as I've ever seen him, as if this game turns him on more than usual.

I lick the head of his cock. He's smooth and salty

and when my lips brush his skin, he jerks in my mouth.

"More."

I take him down my throat, his muffled groans shooting straight between my thighs.

"You want those strangers to know I can't spend an evening with them because I love fucking my student too damned much?"

That shouldn't be hot, but it is. Beyond hot. I'm on fire.

I slide my mouth over him and slide my hand around his shaft.

"Admit that you came here for me," he rasps. "And I'll make this fast."

I pump faster and lick and suck harder.

He fists a hand in my hair, slowing me by force. Every stroke lets him go deeper, and he almost pulls out each time, as if giving me a chance to speak.

His groans are unbearably sexy. "Fuck, I love that mouth wrapped around me. The way you look sucking me off."

When he pushes my head down, holding me by my hair, I feel imminent triumph.

He's breathing so hard I know he's close.

"Coming," he warns. "Don't move."

His whole body goes tight, from his grip on my hair to his abs to his thighs.

When he finishes in my mouth, I swallow every drop.

Eyeliner comes off on my fingers as I swipe at my eyes and rock back on my heels to look at him.

Sawyer's face is cast in shadows, but he's undone. Not his clothes, but him.

He sinks to his knees, his face only a few inches away. Our breath mingles, rapid and shallow, as he strokes a thumb across my cheek with surprising gentleness.

"You're unbelievable," he murmurs. "I don't know what I did to deserve you."

My chest expands until I can't breathe.

"I was going to grab something from the shed, but I looked in the window and there you were and… I couldn't leave without seeing you."

The confession spills out before I can take it back.

His lips ghost over mine, warm and welcoming. As if my words were everything he wanted and more.

I lean in, kissing him back. I'm dizzy and giddy.

On the surface, what just went down was pure wicked sex.

But more than his arousal, I taste his affection.

More than his satisfaction, I feel his commitment.

Every inch of my body is alive with needing to be a part of this man.

What the hell is happening?

My phone buzzes with a text.

Adam: Did you find it?

Liv: Yeah, I'll be right there.

Sawyer's hands skim down my back and cup my ass. "Turn around."

I blink up at him, breathless. "I paid your price."

"That was the price. This is the reward."

My jaw drops. "For what?"

"Admitting you couldn't stay away."

Before I can argue, he spins me around and gives my ass a teasing slap that echoes in the room.

Sawyer lowers the top half of my body to the ground. Then he's dragging my leggings and thong down, leaving them above my knees. The waistband keeps my thighs pressed tight together. Heat floods me, coupled with a sweet ache. I thought we were done, but evidently my dirty professor has another plan.

"You make me crazy. Teasing me with this ass, this pussy."

Is that what he's going to do? Spank me here, so I feel him all night?

Before I can ask, he leans down and kisses the small of my back. He trails his tongue down my crack and I gasp.

"You like how it feels to know that while they're downstairs talking interest rates and estate taxes, I'm taking you an inch at a time?"

Wicked anticipation surges through me, blending with arousal in an intoxicating cocktail. It's filthy and wrong and so hot I might combust.

"You don't want them to hear us, you had better be quiet. If you're too loud I'm going to have to stop. Send you back out there wet and aching."

I nod tightly. There are a lot of ways this could end badly, but that feels like the worst.

"Don't move."

He's gone a moment, then returns. I can't see what he's brought with him, and when he reaches between my legs to stroke my clit, I officially don't care.

It's so good.

I'm rolling my hips, rubbing on his hand.

Sawyer curses as if my reaction is his undoing.

His fingers slip back to my slit. "Take a breath, Cherry."

He presses inside, the thickness of two fingers making me gasp.

Just as my lungs fill with oxygen, I feel it.

There's a buzzing sensation on my clit.

Pleasure rolls over me, one wave spilling into the next. My muscles tighten.

My mouth parts, a silent moan on my lips.

I've definitely never done this, but he makes me bold and brave. I'm longing for something I don't understand, and only Sawyer seems to know how to satisfy the craving.

"So fucking wet for me."

His touch and his words make me arch my back.

He goes deeper, the thrusting of his fingers firm and thick so at odds with the humming.

"Oh my God."

It's illicit tingling that's all the more thrilling because Sawyer knows exactly what he's doing to me.

I already ache for him.

Every jolt of sensation makes my body shake and shiver.

When he withdraws his fingers to slap my ass, I rock into his hand, desperate.

"I think you're ready for more."

More?

His touch withdraws, and I hear the rustle of a packet as he opens a condom and rolls it on.

He leans over and whispers in my ear. "You're unreal like this. On your knees, wet and ready, grinding against my hand even as you arch back, searching for my cock. Do you know which part I like best?"

"No," I manage.

"Me either."

I know how big he feels in my pussy, and the thought of him there with the stimulation on my clit nearly breaks me.

His fingers keep up their torment and his cock bumps against my soaking slit.

The heat of it consumes me. I'm throbbing, my body shaking with anticipation.

"Get ready, sweetheart."

The tip of his cock slides into my opening. I moan.

Loud.

He reaches for the apple on the bed, reaching to hold it in front of my lips.

"Do you trust me?"

Do I?

"Yes."

"Open and bite into this. Wider."

I do as he says and my teeth sink into the apple, my lips pressed against its flesh.

Saliva floods my mouth at the intrusion. But when I try to make a noise, it's muffled against the gag.

Sawyer grips my shoulder, pulling me down on his cock until every inch of him fills me.

I scream but nothing comes out.

"Fuck." His voice drips with pleasure and need.

I twist my face and catch sight of us in the floor length mirror in the corner. He's too hot. We're too hot. I'm an inferno, melting down from the inside out.

Our gazes connect, his mouth parted, eyes hooded.

But the second I swear I can't handle it, he reassures me with his eyes and hands and body.

We're riding this edge together.

He starts off slow, but it doesn't last. The moment I start to relax he knows. He fucks me with deep, sure thrusts.

I fight the pressure against my clit as every nerve inside me is on fire.

He bites my neck and my body goes rigid, my orgasm exploding.

He rides me through my release, grinding in and

out of me, and then when I feel him coming, his cock jerks.

His body shakes with his own release and I slump to the carpet.

I'm boneless.

Floating.

A woman reborn in skin that's too thin and new.

But at the same time, I know unequivocally that I was made for this.

Sawyer leans over me, all dark satisfaction with a hint of concern as he reaches for the apple and helps work it out of my mouth. I start to rub my jaw, but he moves my hand away and does it for me.

"You okay?"

"Better than okay."

He helps me up to standing. I'm sore and used and delicious, but I wouldn't take it back.

Not for anything.

I reach for my underwear and leggings and tug them up. My phone is on the bed somehow, and when I grab it, I spot the half dozen messages.

"Shit. I'm so late."

Sawyer straightens his clothes, chuckling.

He drags my face up to his and kisses me, long and deep.

"That's for crashing my party." Sawyer's thumb

brushes my lower lip, as if he's tracing the path of his mouth. "I missed you tonight, too."

My heart kicks in my chest, because the confession feels like so much more.

"You want to stay for a drink?"

"Just had one," I say.

His mouth curves. "You know what I mean."

But I can't. We both know it.

I need to go back to my world and he needs to stay here in his.

He walks me downstairs and I take the telescope.

"We used to look at the stars with that," Sawyer says.

My chest aches. "Really? I can't—"

"Take it." He pushes it into my grip, closes my hands around it. "Build something amazing."

When I get back out to my team, Adam's on his phone and Madison's pacing.

"What the hell took so long?" Royce demands.

I cut a look at Madison, but she's facing away—on purpose or by accident, I'm not sure.

"We found something else we needed." Adam holds up a rake.

"Where'd you get that?"

"Across the street."

I look over toward Daniel's house. "That one?"

"Yup."

Crap.

"Did he—they," I amend, "see you?"

Adam smirks. "Nah, we've got mad skills, Liv."

The front door opens, and Daniel's there.

"What are you..."

He spots the rake in our hands.

Then pulls on shoes and comes after us.

"Do something!" Madison hisses.

"You do something!" I retort, because he'll recognize me.

Madison flashes him.

I can't believe it.

We're laughing the entire way to my car.

"Thanks to you, we're way behind," Madison says, breathless, when she catches up. "We have an hour to get back to campus."

The sixty minutes are a strange kind of bliss.

We drive around town, grabbing whatever we can, being young and alive.

It's a different kind of freedom than I felt with Sawyer. With him, I still felt safe to explore because I knew he had me.

Here, it's only us.

When I notice the time, I grab Madison's arm. "We have fifteen minutes to get back!"

"We can't get the last item."

"Yes, we can."

I run back to the car, and Adam's in the driver's seat.

"Get in," he hollers.

We do, Madison and Royce piling into the back and me leaping into the passenger seat. I'm still grabbing for my seat belt when Adam peels out of our spot, racing down the street.

"Glad you came?" he demands.

"Only if we get back in time to build our tower."

"Better than being yelled at about basketball."

"By your coach or your dad?"

"Both. Coach wants more of my time. Dad wants me to quit."

Empathy rises up, and I shift in my seat.

I kick something in the passenger side and bend to pick it up.

It's a bottle of liquor.

Numbness washes over me. "Adam? What the fuck is this?"

"Slow down!" Madison yelps.

I brace against the glove compartment with one hand, still fishing for the seat belt with the other.

Two tiny glowing orbs light up the road in front of us.

A cat? A dog?

My throat tightens. "Adam! Look out!"

He swerves, his hands jerking on the wheel.

Too late.

Tires screech.

Lights blind me from my window.

The crunch of metal and plastic sounds like it's coming from inside my head.

The world slams into me.

Everything goes black.

17

SAWYER

"They're interested in putting in an offer," the realtor murmurs at my back.

"A productive evening."

The soft hand on my arm has me looking up from where I'm staring out the front window, watching the last of the people leave.

"You disappeared for a long time after you told me not to let anyone upstairs."

"Had to attend to something."

A young woman in black leggings sucking me off from her knees.

I made sure no one was going to interrupt us, but didn't need Olivia to know that.

"Tonight doesn't have to be over." The realtor eyes me appreciatively.

"You're clearly very good at your job, and you're an attractive woman, but there's someone in my life."

"Is it serious?"

She made me promise no feelings.

Promises are made to be broken.

Especially after what went down an hour ago.

"Yeah."

The realtor sighs. "I figured. It's too bad she couldn't come tonight."

She did.

The other woman nods to the bowl of apples on the foyer table. "Can I take one for the road?"

"Help yourself."

All I can think about is the girl who came in here tonight like a punk.

Until she arrived, it was a boring evening with boring people. I actually imagined her here with me more than once.

When she appeared, face flushed with guilt and longing, I couldn't believe my eyes.

I never got anything I wished for before.

I needed her to admit she couldn't stay away from me, either.

She should've been at my side downstairs, making comments under her breath and straightening out-of-place decor and blushing every time she looked at those apples.

"So is she moving to New York with you when you go?"

The question throws me.

I never let myself hope for more, but now...

She's not a kid. She's an adult, and not only because of what we did upstairs.

Olivia helped me prepare for tonight. She's mature enough to make her own choices.

My phone rings and I grab for it when I see the name on the screen. "Hello? Olivia?"

The realtor's eyebrows rise.

"Sawyer." Her voice is panting. "We were driving back to campus and it happened so fast."

Every muscle in me tightens. "Are you hurt? What happened? Where are you?"

She gives me an intersection. "The ambulance is here. Adam was driving. He was...I think he was drinking."

Fuck.

I watch my words when I hang up. "I have to go."

Jaw set, I head outside and get into the car.

A ten-minute drive never passed this slowly. My knuckles turn white on the steering wheel.

When I arrive at the scene, they're loading her car onto a tow truck. Not one but two police cars and an ambulance are there, sirens blinking.

I wrench the car to the side of the road and leap out, leaving the door open.

I spot Olivia first, her hair a mess and eyes round with shock.

"What the hell..." I start.

I want to drag her into my arms but I have to shake myself. I can't. Not here in front of Madison and Royce, hanging their heads by the curb.

"What's going on?" I demand of the officer nearby.

"They were street racing," he replies.

Not drinking and driving.

I see a breathalyzer apparatus in one of his hands. They must have checked Adam and he must have passed. I feel an ounce of relief, but nowhere near enough.

I might be reckless, but this is inexcusable.

"Where is Adam?"

She nods to the ambulance. "He hurt his arm on impact."

Sure enough, I can see paramedics working on someone in the bright lights of the vehicle.

"Something ran in front of the car. A deer, I think."

"How fast were you going?"

Olivia turns away but Madison answers.

"Pretty fast. We hit another car. Everyone in it was okay."

I turn back to the officer.

"They weren't street racing," I force myself to say. "It was an engineering event."

"And you are?"

"Sawyer Redmond. Professor Sawyer Redmond. These are my students."

"This was a school initiative?"

My throat is tight with disgust. "An unsanctioned one."

The officer pulls up his belt. "We need to finish our investigation. There may be criminal charges pending."

"They're kids. They were stupid and careless."

In the corner of my eye, Olivia pulls her knees tighter into her chest.

"Just a moment," the officer says, departing to speak with a colleague standing at the flashing cruiser.

"What were you thinking?" I hiss at all of them, but my gaze is locked on Olivia.

Madison is the one who answers, her voice shaky. "We were going to miss getting back to campus by the deadline."

I rub a hand over my face, catching sight of

Olivia's wrecked Audi being loaded onto a tow truck bed.

Unbelievable.

They could have been hurt, or worse.

I could have lost her over some idiot prank.

I never got any handouts in my life. These students have had everything they could want—money, opportunity.

This is a lesson they need to learn.

Royce's face is downcast, his fingers drumming on his knee shakily. Madison rocks back and forth. And Olivia's got a blanket around her shoulders.

I start to turn away, but see a dark splotch on Madison's temple in the streetlight.

"Are you hurt?" I grab her chin and tilt her head.

"It's a scrape."

"Anyone else? Olivia?" I turn to her.

She shakes her head slowly, but when she moves to re-wrap the blanket around her shoulders, I spot a rip in the side of her shirt—the one I hung onto a few hours ago.

When the officer returns, I wave him over. "They need medical attention."

"Medics are finishing up with the other kid, said everyone was okay—"

"Then why is there blood on them?" My voice rises.

Adam appears, his arm bound in a sling as he shuffles over. His face has scratches, possibly from the impact of the airbag deploying.

"Here's what's going to happen," I grit out. "You let them go home—all of them. You need any more statements, you can get them in the morning."

"We'd rather take them tonight."

"They'll sleep in their beds tonight. They've had the living shit scared out of them, and by the looks of them, worse than that. You think I'm up your ass, you have no idea what kind of a stink their parents are going to cause."

We head to my car without waiting for an answer.

We're halfway there when Royce blows out a breath. "Professor Redmond, that was—"

"Shut up."

"Wait." Olivia cranes her neck to see the tow truck starting up. "I need to get stuff from my car."

"Leave it," I say, exasperated, but Olivia runs back in that direction, speaking to the driver.

The other students follow her and she passes out the items they borrowed for the event. They pile into my car, along with half a dozen tools, toys, and my dad's telescope. Olivia shifts into the back between Madison and Royce. Adam takes the front, sliding in gingerly to avoid hitting his arm.

"Doesn't look like you'll be playing basketball for a while."

He doesn't answer.

We drive in silence. I sneak a look in the rearview mirror; the streetlights run over their faces in the dark.

Olivia looks shaken and guilty and too damn young, her arms wrapped around the telescope.

I focus back on the road. "That rake looks like the one my neighbor Daniel has."

Madison shifts lower in her seat.

Olivia's gaze flicks toward her, the first sign of life. Adam coughs and Royce grumbles.

I did all I could by coming down here to get them.

It doesn't feel like enough.

Why the fuck doesn't it feel like enough?

My hands clench and relax on the steering wheel.

"When I did Black Build, we came in last, even though we had the tallest tower."

Someone in the back seat shifts.

"Why?" Royce asks.

"We weren't allowed to use anything...borrowed."

"But now you're encouraged to. There's no way to get full marks if you don't."

Madison this time.

"You could've taken the stolen stuff out."

Olivia's voice is barely more than a whisper, but the knot in my chest releases a degree.

"That wasn't the point."

Streetlights pass, illuminating rows of tidy, expensive houses that line the streets bordering campus.

"Build it anyway," I hear myself say.

Royce straightens. "It won't count."

"You're engineers. You don't build things because someone offered you points to do it. Build it anyway."

They exchange looks.

"We have all the stuff," Royce concedes.

Olivia nods. "We'd just have to stash it some-where for the night otherwise. What do you think?" She reaches for the good shoulder of the kid sitting numb and silent in the seat next to me.

He doesn't acknowledge for a long time.

But finally he nods.

18

———

SAWYER

"**W**hy is my rake in the middle of a statue?" Daniel demands during our run through campus early Monday morning.

I lift my phone to take a picture. "You're part of history, my friend."

I send the image to Olivia.

Sawyer: Looks good in the light of day.

Cherry: Better than me.

Sawyer: How are you feeling?

. . .

Cherry: Like I was in a car accident.

Fucking Adam. But she had to file reports and is waiting on the insurance company's valuation of the damage.

Still, being there for them was the right thing to do.

I was pissed at all of them for being reckless. Was that what my father felt like with me?

I hated that I couldn't grab her by the arms and shake her, tell her she was insane.

Kiss her to make sure she was all right.

Sawyer: Stop by after your midterm.

I haven't seen her since I dropped them off here Saturday night to work on their tower. I need to see for myself that she's unharmed.

Cherry: You'll see me in class.

.   .   .

Sawyer: Insufficient, Miss Barclay. I'll get lunch. With chips. We'll eat in my office.

"Any action on your house?" Daniel asks as we head across campus, him to his office, me to mine.

I pocket my phone. "An offer came in, but we can do better."

"But if you close during winter break, you can leave by next year. Unless you want to stay and you're looking for excuses."

"Of course not. The plan is to leave at the first opportunity. In six months, I'll be building something new. Leave all this behind, go back to my life. Friends in New York."

Strange that I don't miss New York much.

"You want to walk away from her like nothing happened."

No. I don't want to walk away from her at all.

Seeing her in an accident scared the shit out of me, because it made real the possibility I could lose her.

I love having her around. I want to protect her. Be with her.

I think she wants the same thing. But I need her to admit it.

I collect my belongings from my office and head to class.

Olivia's there, and every time I scan the students, I linger an extra beat on her. It's instinctual, I can't stop it.

She's got a bruise on her face and I want to erase it.

Or kill the kid in the row behind her wearing a sling who keeps sending her looks like he's sorry.

I grip the marker so hard it's a wonder the thing doesn't explode all over the whiteboard.

When I ask a question about circuits, Liv's hand goes up, and Madison's.

"Adam. I'll spare you the discomfort of raising your hand, but assume you have an answer."

He straightens in his seat, looking at his papers. "Ahh…"

"Any day now."

"I'm not sure."

"You want to live dangerously, incompetence isn't the way to do it."

I turn back to the front.

After the lecture, I'm cleaning off the whiteboard when motion at my side has me looking over.

"Are you okay?" Olivia wipes off the second board, pressing up on her toes to reach the top. "That was harsh."

I drop my eraser and step closer to inspect her face. "This must hurt."

"Only a little." Her hand wraps around my wrist, and that small contact grounds me. I huff out a breath.

We're in the middle of a classroom.

I lower my hand.

"So now you've seen me. Does this mean I don't need to come to your office, Professor?" she teases.

"Not a chance."

I watch her leave, the sway of her hips calling to me.

Yeah, I'm gone for this girl. And I need to know she feels the same.

When I get back to the department, I notice that the elevator's operating.

About damned time things were going right around here.

"Mother trucker..." comes a female voice from the staff and faculty kitchen.

I poke my head inside the door where Betty's wrestling with the coffee maker.

"Takedown at the ten-yard line?"

"Something like that." She grimaces as she stabs at the "start" button. The machine offers only stubborn silence. "It probably needs cleaning."

I wave her off and set to work.

A couple of junior faculty come in the door, groaning when they see the state of the coffee maker. "Five minutes," Betty promises.

They retreat and I roll up the sleeves of my dress shirt.

"You're good with your hands, Professor." Her teasing tone makes me grin. "Oh, I know what you're thinking. But I'm twenty years too old to find out. Fine, thirty."

"Any man would be so lucky."

"Charmer. It's going to be a long day. Industry members are visiting campus. It's been on the calendar for weeks, and the dean's way to drum up interest in our graduates—as well as potential funding sooner."

"He didn't invite me to any meetings. I must be bad publicity."

"No, he probably thinks you'd steal his attention."

I finish my work and tell Betty to run the cycle again.

She does and the machine whirrs to life.

I roll my sleeves back down. "All this for worse coffee than the cafeteria."

"It's not the best but it's what we've got."

It's what we've got.

I cross to the kitchen window, taking in the packs of two and three and four jacket-clad undergrads drifting across the expanse of green and paved walk-ways. "Some students got in trouble at Black Build this weekend."

"I did hear about that. Most of the department heard about it," she concedes. "There was an article in the news, and it made the campus paper too. Didn't help they're all sporting bruises and scrapes."

"They crashed a car in the middle of town."

If Olivia's right, there was an animal running across the road. But if they'd been doing the speed limit, it could've been handled. Easily.

"You're all worked up because they were *your* kids."

I shake my head. "They're not my kids."

"They are. You get attached to them. And they fuck up," she says. "They're lucky to have you."

I glance back over my shoulder. "Why's that?"

"You show them it's possible to grow and change at any age. This place is changing you. Like it changed your father."

"I never saw him change. That's why I left."

Betty lifts a mug to her lips, sipping the coffee and considering me over the rim. "That's what changed him."

Before I can respond, an unwelcome shape appears at the door.

"Sawyer. We have a special guest," the dean says,

but it's the man in a suit next to him that has my abs tightening in surprise.

"Tate." My voice echoes in my ears. "I didn't realize you were part of industry day."

He clasps my hand in his. "I wasn't but he called personally yesterday and insisted I participate. Sent a car and everything."

What the fuck?

"He wanted to meet some of our finest students firsthand," the dean goes on, the smugness coming off as pride. "Including yours."

That's it. He wants to make me look bad in front of Tate. He's trying to ruin me the way he thinks I hurt him.

"Your dean was kind enough to distribute an email to third- and fourth-year students giving them time slots to meet," Tate goes on. "I asked him to start with your Stars team. I can't wait to see the impression you've had on them since we last met."

19

OLIVIA

Our tower is amazing. I stop in front of the engineering building and smile.

After my midterm, I head to Sawyer's office for lunch.

His irritated expression dissolves when he spots me. "Everything okay?"

I shut the door behind me.

"Well, my history midterm went all right but I have two labs to turn in before the end of the week, and this panel to speak on, and we need to write and rehearse the justification presentation for Stars."

Sawyer surprises me as he bends to claim my lips with his.

It's possessive and searching and I reach up and run my fingers through his hair.

"We need to talk," he says when he pulls back.

"Yeah. I guess we do."

We haven't touched since Saturday night at his open house, and I'm aching for him.

Our encounter was super hot, but when he came to get us after the accident, he was distant.

Not that I expected him to grab me in front of my classmates, but the look in his eyes was removed. I couldn't tell if he was angry or shaken or both.

A knock on the door makes me stiffen.

Sawyer steps back and opens it.

It's Tate.

Sawyer's friend from New York is familiar in a dark suit, his hair neatly trimmed and smile warm yet professional.

"Good, you're both here. I'm hoping to speak to you. Especially you, Miss Barclay." His smile fades as he takes in my bruise. "Did something happen?"

I duck my face. "No. Just a prank gone wrong."

He clears his throat, but the wariness lingers. "I'm not sure how much your professor has told you, but we have plans for a new effort."

Sawyer returns to his desk. Tate sinks into the chair opposite him.

I don't know what script I'm supposed to follow, so I take the remaining seat.

"I understand you're going into business together."

People pass in the hall.

I stick out my legs, my feet slipping under the edge of the desk. It feels weird that I can't touch Sawyer.

"Yes. I was very impressed with your adaptability at regionals," Tate goes on. "Your grades are strong, but more than that, creativity and working under pressure are integral to being a good engineer. Which is why you should consider us for your internship in the summer."

"Excuse me?"

My gaze flies to Sawyer's.

Did he and Tate talk about this?

"I'm not confident that's in our collective best interest," Sawyer says smoothly.

Tate frowns. "Do you have an internship already? We can offer an excellent package."

My mouth opens and closes. I hadn't really considered where I'd intern. Adam said he'd have room at his parents' company, but I'd rather work somewhere else.

"Olivia—may I call you Olivia?" Tate asks.

"Of course."

Professor Redmond calls me whatever he wants when he's fucking me.

"I understand you might be concerned with a potential conflict..."

The floor tilts under me.

"...because Professor Redmond is responsible for your grade. But it won't affect that. Sawyer, tell her."

"To be frank, Tate, I'm not sure this is the right fit for everyone."

Hurt seeps into my chest, stinging. "I assure you, Professor Redmond, I'm as capable as any intern you'd hope to find."

His eyes flash in warning. "And while I appreciate your flexibility"—my brows lift—"there's more to success than that."

"Sawyer! For God's sake, you are the worst recruiter." Tate glowers. "I have another meeting. But think about it," he says to me before rising and heading for the door. "If you'd like to talk, I'll be around. Here's my card."

He spares us a final look on the way out, leaving us alone, the door still open.

"What was that?" Sawyer demands once Tate is gone.

"You tell me. It's your business partner who sprung this on me." Sawyer's words about this being a bad fit echo in my mind. "Am I that terrible, you wouldn't consider me for an internship at your company?"

"Of course I would. But we can't work together."

"Because of rumors from your last company?"

"Because anyone could take one look at us and know I'm..." He rubs a hand over his jaw.

My heart thuds in my chest. "You're what?"

Sleeping with me?

There are words I suddenly want him to say, ones I've never dared hope for.

Say this is as real and right as it is crazy.

Say when you close your eyes, it's me you see.

Say we have a chance to not only be free, but to be happy.

But I'm trying to make my own way, not jump from being under my parents' control to under this man's. It's one thing for him to have my back, another to depend on him for my security, my future.

"You'd be working *for* me," he says, softer. "You think there's a gap now, it'll be even more obvious when you're a junior engineer and I'm running the company."

"Or we'd stop doing what we're doing."

I'm not making a suggestion, only enumerating the other obvious option, but his gaze sharpens.

My stomach flips, as if I'm staring down a long hill, treacherously steep.

"I mean," I stumble on, "summer's a long time away. And my future is important to me. If I have to choose, maybe I'd rather work with you than..."

"Fuck me."

That doesn't sound right. It doesn't feel right either.

Yes, we're sleeping together, yet it's so much more than that.

But he's staring so intently, I nod.

"Fine," he bites out. "So we'd stop."

He says it as if it's easy for him to turn it off, what we're doing. A decision made in a heartbeat.

I'm tumbling down the hill now, the ground slamming into me everywhere.

"Is that what you want?" I ask, struggling for breath.

Sawyer's hands grip the armrests of his chair.

I get that there's a legit concern about conflict of interests.

The truth is, I can't see myself looking at him every day and not want to be with him.

He reaches into his drawer and produces a brown paper bag—lunch, probably.

Our hands brush. His touch lingers, his thumb stroking the back of my knuckles.

"Let's just focus on what's happening now," he murmurs. "If the Stars team does well in the justification and makes it to finals, you can write your own ticket."

"Do you have an extra pen?" I ask Madison in class that afternoon.

"I don't think so."

Her voice is tight and dismissive.

"How's midterm death week going?" She doesn't answer and I glance down at my outfit. "I have matching socks, so...could be worse."

She shakes her head.

"Want to meet up and talk about our submission for the justification panel?" I say. "It's only three weeks away, and we need to wow them."

"It's not over, is it?" She turns toward me, eyes flashing. "You and Professor Redmond. I saw the way you looked at each other that night in the car."

No matter her role in distributing the video from Velvet, she doesn't deserve lies.

"I can't stay away from him," I admit. "It is causing problems, though not in the way you think." Madison waits me out. "Professor Redmond's partner offered me an internship. At their new company in New York."

"Of course he did." She shifts in her seat, tugging at a chunk of red hair as if focusing all her attention on it might make it combust.

"What would you do?" I ask.

"I'd take it," she says immediately. "Take it, but

make sure you cover your ass so there's no way he can fire you if the thing between you goes south."

I don't want to cover my ass with Sawyer. I want to trust him completely.

"Have you looked at internships for the summer?" I ask.

"I'm going to work with Engineers without Borders. When I was a kid, we went to visit a developing country. A building burned down because the work wasn't done right. I want to do jobs right, and anyone who doesn't do them right should be exposed. People should be free to live their lives without worrying about their own safety."

"That's amazing."

"Everyone has their own reason. No one's is better than anyone else's. That's just mine." She shrugs. "So we'll work on the justification tomorrow?"

"Can we do it the next day? I have to speak on a panel about women in engineering school." I explain how I met Aliya on the call and she invited me to participate.

"You're exactly who they want. Perfect spokesperson. Stick you in a hardhat and you're a stock photo."

"Stock photos don't hold up very well in real life. Can they build a circuit or write code? I don't think so."

She rolls her eyes, but her lips twitch.

"Hey," I decide, impulsive. "Why don't you do it with me?"

"Because they asked you and it's weird to have two people."

"So?"

The professor starts to lecture and a moment later, there's a nudge at my elbow.

Madison's pen.

"We're going to look stupid," she whispers.

I grin.

20

———

OLIVIA

Madison and I use a conference room in the library the next day and share my notebook computer screen to participate in the roundtable. Our shoulders bump when we answer questions from excited high school juniors and sophs about class, student life, careers.

I grew up with a sister who loved me. But Madison makes me work for every ounce of it.

When that icy chill melts a little, I realize how good it feels to be respected by someone who has no reason to respect me.

When we wrap up and wave goodbye, I head across the rolling hills of campus toward my apartment, the early afternoon breeze cooling my cheeks.

I think back to Tate's internship offer.

I can't picture reporting to the man I'm falling for, but working in his company could be exciting. I believe in him and his vision. He's endlessly capable, and I can't imagine him working with people who aren't.

Plus, it would mean being in New York with Sawyer for the entire summer.

In the moments when I'm lying in bed alone in my dorm room, I think about waking up next to him.

I want to argue over snack foods and games and the state of the world as we walk through Midtown.

To elbow him in the gut when he gripes about someone being ridiculous when they're only being human.

To tangle my fingers in his hair while he uses his smug mouth to take me apart one layer at a time, because when his tongue is inside me, it's the only thing that matters.

My phone vibrates, and I hope it's Sawyer, but it's not.

Mom: We need the car back tonight.

· · ·

I haven't heard from the insurance adjuster, so I call them. By the time I get through to the person on my file, I'm opening the door of our apartment.

"Olivia, we just received a valuation for your car."

"Valuation. You mean how much it's going to cost to fix."

"The car is totalled. Not worth fixing. I can tell you how much we'll give you for it."

The door clicks shut behind me as they name a figure, but my ears are buzzing so much I barely hear.

My beautiful car is toast.

The good girl side of me is ashamed. Even though it was Adam who crashed the car, some small part of me knew this was going to be a crazy night.

But the rest of me chafes against my mom's demand that I give them back the car in its entirety.

I worked for that money.

"Olivia? Does that sound reasonable? We can cut you a check tomorrow."

Which my mom will try to confiscate.

I start to say yes, but nothing comes out.

My fingers grasp for my necklace—the one I gave away in a moment of inspired insanity.

The one Sawyer got back for me.

Some rules are meant to be followed, especially if they protect us and those around us.

But life has too many contingencies, and not many rules are equipped to handle them.

Doing what's right doesn't mean saying yes.

"Actually," I start, "it was in new condition. And it had upgraded trim."

The man on the other end pauses. "I see."

"Plus there were snow tires on it. Expensive ones."

He clicks away on his computer. "We can do an extra twenty-five hundred."

I savor the small victory as I make arrangements to get the check and hang up.

I'm going to need it after I show up at home without the car.

In Manhattan, I get off the Amtrak and take the subway.

I let myself in the front door and nearly trip over boxes.

"What's going on?" I call as I step out of my boots and unfurl my scarf. I head for the kitchen where my mother appears in the doorway.

"Doing some fall cleaning. Your father's at the office." She brushes past me to look out the front living room window, her tailored black pants and a white silk shirt hugging her body.

"Did you bring the car?"

I frown. "The car is totalled."

Mom starts to brush the hair behind her ear, then stops. "Excuse me?"

"We were doing a school thing, Adam was driving and…it doesn't matter. They're cutting me a check, which I'm going to cash. I'll take the amount I earned from it, and the extra I negotiated, and transfer you the rest."

I expect her to fight me but her shoulders slump. She turns and heads down the hall for her room.

I follow her there and pull up when I see the costumes lying across the bed, from her performances. "What are these doing out?"

Maybe she's looking at them, remembering her career as a dancer. The same one she wanted for me, that I couldn't deliver.

"I'm auctioning them off."

"For charity?"

"For us."

I drop onto the bed next to a tutu in a garment bag. "It's that bad."

She heads for her closet and pulls open the door.

From here, I can see empty hangers. "Where are all your clothes?"

"They went first," comes the tight voice. "I sold them before the costumes."

Damn.

She's not only asking me to sell the car. Evidently, this is one in a line of sacrifices.

I get up and pad toward the closet, finding my mother kneeling inside, a hand pressed to her face.

"What does Emma think of all this?"

"She doesn't know the extent of it. I've tried to keep it from her. I don't want her worrying."

"But you put it all on me."

"Because you can handle it." My mother rises and squares her shoulders. "Have a drink with me."

There's a first for everything. To my knowledge, she never drinks except at social events.

I lead the way to the kitchen, where she hunts through the wine fridge.

"When I got pregnant with you," she starts, getting down on her knees to pull out bottles and check labels, "I didn't expect it. I was a twenty-four-year-old dancer. By having a child at that age, I'd be giving up my career. I wanted a better life for you. Hence marrying your father."

"I thought you were engaged when you had me."

"We were. He had ideas of being a free man for longer. I disabused him of that notion."

"What are you looking for?"

"Special bottle," she grunts. "We were saving it for our twentieth wedding anniversary. Or I was. Instead of drinking it, he was caught up with work."

I kneel next to her, pulling out bottles for her to inspect.

"He didn't want to take responsibility at first. I wanted to be sure you would have the security I didn't. I wanted you to be taken care of always."

The next bottle has her exclaiming. "Voilà."

She rises gracefully, and I reach for two crystal glasses from the cupboard. We take everything out to the terrace of the townhouse.

She pours her own the same size, then adds another half an inch to the crystal before setting the bottle down on a table.

"Men can fuck you over. I don't ever want that for you. I wanted to protect you from it, but it seems I have less control than I thought."

She takes a long sip of her wine.

"Promise me you won't let that happen."

I was a whole person before Sawyer Redmond. With dreams and likes and dislikes.

Was I though?

It feels as if I was half awake, as if everything I did was conditional upon what other people wanted and decided I should want and be and have. If someone liberates you rather than you liberating yourself, does it mean you're still trapped, just in different surroundings?

"I promise."

I'm going to prove her wrong. There's no way Sawyer's going to let me down.

21

———

SAWYER

Cherry: You get something to eat this morning?

Sawyer: Yes, but I want another taste tonight.

The past two weeks we've settled into a routine. She stays at my place a couple of nights a week. She feeds the fish, indulges my crazy ideas, and I take care of her.

Make sure she's eating. Make sure she's coming.

We spend every second we can steal together, and I love making her laugh, and she makes this cute face when she's about to call me on my bullshit.

I've made it my personal mission to push her, but lately, she's more than meeting me.

This morning I got up to find her stretching next to the bed. She looked so damned beautiful I didn't want to disturb her, but I couldn't resist wrapping my arms around her body and running my hands up beneath her tank top. When she moaned and leaned back into me, I lay back and pulled her over me.

The old Olivia would've let me do it.

The new Olivia stripped the tank top off, put her hands in her hair, and arched her back like a cat while she held my eyes through the slits of hers.

Fucking yes.

I've been more careful around campus, but when she came in to talk about the project, I couldn't resist threading my fingers through hers. The team is getting closer to accomplishing something real and meaningful, and I'm beyond proud.

This started out with me wanting to take a few layers off her perfection and show her the world is better when you let go.

Now, I'm falling for the way her mind works. I love that she wants to save the world, even if that world is a place I didn't care much for until I knew she was part of it.

Still, she's holding a piece of herself back.

When Tate proposed her working for us, the idea seemed insane. But the more I think about it, the more I like it.

What I don't like is how easily she suggested we could end what's between us if it meant her getting an internship.

Cherry: Shit. Shit shit shit.

The message comes as I make my way across the hill to the engineering department.

Sawyer: You and the team working late today?

Cherry: Yes. We're behind and it's my fault.

Sawyer: I doubt that.

But I hit her contact.

"Stars took my name off the updates list when I was late for that informational call," Olivia says on a whoosh of breath. "So there's a whole extra section we have to submit that no one told us about. I tried booking lab time but the schedule said it was full."

"Let me see what I can do."

"You're the best. Anything I can bring tomorrow for dinner?"

"I have caterers. Just show up, along with the other fifty people."

"I can do that." She sighs. "Thanks, Sawyer."

"You got it, sweetheart."

I click off, an extra bounce in my stride as I head through the front doors and up the stairs to the second floor.

I'm hosting a pre-finals social for half the department. Evidently one of the faculty hosts every year, and I drew the short stick, being new and all.

No matter I'm only here temporarily.

I was going to beg off, but Olivia suggested I go through with it to show everyone I'm playing ball.

By the administration desk I pause, pulling out my phone and typing out an impulse text.

Sawyer: There is one thing you can do. Wear that skirt I like.

"Let me guess: you've been summoned?"

I glance up at Betty's voice. "Looks that way."

"Here you go. The mid-semester student

reviews." She holds them out and I accept them. "In case the dean gives you shit for them. He'll use anything to dig at you."

"I can take him."

She winces, and it occurs to me that when I piss him off, it probably makes things harder on people I care about. Ones who don't deserve his bullshit but can't walk away like I can.

I skim the feedback.

The only lectures I don't skip.

Tough but knows what he's talking about.

Seems like a different guy from the start of the semester.

My brows lift. "They like me."

"You don't have to sound so surprised. Your father was secretly delighted when he had good reviews."

My laughter fades. "I have a hard time picturing that."

In the past couple weeks, I've gone through some of my dad's old things, and I'm starting to see what Olivia meant—he seems like a different person since I left.

I'm not ready to let him off the hook for how he raised me, but knowing he was a better man after I left stings less than I thought it would.

Still thinking of Olivia's request, I pull up my

phone and look at the lab schedule. Sure enough, the entire day is blocked out. "Hey. How can I see who's using the lab? It usually shows who's in it."

Betty leans over to look at my phone. "That means a central booking from the dean's office. Except I'm usually the one to make the booking. Let me check..." She turns to her computer, entering a few keystrokes. "We had cameras installed in the main lab after a prank break-in last year. Except...the lab's empty."

It makes zero sense.

My grip on the phone tightens as a text message displays on a banner across the screen between us.

Cherry: You like any skirt without anything underneath, Professor.

Betty's gaze meets mine.

Fuck.

I clear my throat. "It's not..."

"What it looks like?"

That hangs between us.

"I want you to be happy, Sawyer. Happy doesn't always mean following the rules, behaving like society expects us to. But…" She goes on, inhaling sharply, "Not everyone is as open-minded."

The door behind her opens and the dean appears. "Professor Redmond. Come in. Have a seat."

He's powerful on this campus, and dangerous. He can't ruin my life, but he would get off trying, and he'd ruin a lot of other people that I care about.

So I sit in the chair facing his desk while he claims the one behind it.

"You tried to fuck me over," I start.

"Excuse me?"

"By inviting Tate here to meet my students after Black Build. It didn't work, and it won't."

"Whatever you're imagining, it's pure conjecture. Now, we're talking about your reviews." He shuffles papers on his desk. "Faculty can't return if their reviews aren't satisfactory."

I cross my arms. "We both know this was a one-time-only thing. Covering for Lancaster until you can hire someone new."

He cocks his head, surprised. "Surely you at least want to apply. Do you have any idea how many faculty would kill for this job?"

I want to tell him where to stick his invitation, but Betty's warning echoes in my head. Pissing him off more than necessary will only make life harder for people I care about, including her. She'll have to deal with his scorched ego when I walk out of here.

He clears his throat. "You scored a four point oh out of five. This is below the departments' goal of a four point three review from all faculty."

"If I'm not mistaken, your reviews last semester were a three point six."

"How did you..." He turns so red he's nearly purple.

I lean over his desk, picking up an expensive-looking pen on the blotter. "I have an agenda item, too. I want the faculty's full support for my Stars team. No phantom lab bookings that don't exist."

He grabs the pen from my hand. "It's an indulgent exercise. We could be investing in faculty instead of—"

"Students? We're a university. What the fuck else should we be investing in?"

"It's a research institution! This department has the opportunity to produce leading innovations."

"And you're afraid those new ideas will come from the students, not from you."

He wants success, but only if he can take all the credit. If my team does well, that credit goes to them, and perhaps to me. He can't stand it.

Students are the lifeblood of this and every

school. Faculty's job is to help them learn from their mistakes, but it's not a place to find your own glory.

"You have no idea the pressures we're under. You never wanted to be here," he sputters. "Even as a student, you thought you were too good for this place. So what changed? You didn't suddenly start caring for these students. You only care about yourself. Lancaster took you in because he felt obliged. He thought he could tame you, make something of you. But you're a wild animal no one else wanted."

The accusations glance off me as I rise from my seat.

"The students are presenting to the justification committee in another week. I expect no further interference, unless you want this elevated to the provost's office. I'm sure the university would be glad to ensure the team is appropriately supported if engineering is struggling." I reach into the inside pocket of my jacket to pull out a flyer and set it in front of him. "I hope we'll see you at the party."

22

OLIVIA

"You look like you could use this after all the hours we've been pulling this week." Adam brings me a drink from the long table the caterers set up in Lancaster's backyard.

"Thanks." I take the cup and sip. The cider fits the fall vibe, though it's unseasonably warm enough I'm wearing a denim jacket and Adam's in his team jacket from basketball.

"How's the arm holding up?" I nod to Adam's shoulder, still in a bandage from the accident.

"It's healing, but I'm off basketball."

"I'm sorry. But it could have been worse. When I found that bottle…I was scared you were drinking."

"I had it with me, but only had a sip. And not in the car," he goes on at my look. "It was a mistake. I seem to be making them a lot. But I hope I haven't made any I can't come back from."

"Meaning?"

"There are things you get over, and ones you can't." He shoves his good hand through his hair. "It's been a rough semester. But we survived, right? Just a week until finals."

We toast, his cup to mine.

"Couldn't see Redmond hosting a party before. At least one like this."

I follow Adam's gaze to Sawyer, who's deigning to make small talk with other faculty. He's dressed in dark jeans and a sweater, nodding as if he's trying to stay invested in the conversation when he's secretly itching to bolt.

I have a plan—one that starts with everyone, including Sawyer, having a good time.

I told Sawyer it would be smart for the department to see him like this, but it's more than that.

The past couple of weeks have been amazing. Neither of us has brought up the future and a possible internship. But pressure for the competition is dialing up, and my mom's words linger in the back of my mind.

"I bet the guy's done some crazy shit in his life. That's why you're so hot for him."

I cough, some of my drink going down the wrong way. "Excuse me?"

"His influence is all over the justification."

Relief edges in. It makes sense that his ideas would creep in, because we've been talking about it —not only after class, but at night in bed and over dinner a couple times when I've hitched a ride back here with Daniel and Andy after dance class.

"Plus that stuff about underwater reclamation," Adam continues. "You really want to save the world?"

"You're going to inherit a company someday. Do you want to use it to leave the world better than before?"

A dozen feet away, Madison's eyeing Royce, who's being obtuse as usual.

Across the yard, Betty's throwing a football with some grad students.

We might each have our own weirdness, but we're together. People are celebrating a beautiful day in a beautiful place at the kind of university most kids dream of attending.

"I don't know, Liv. Maybe we can try." His frown deepens and he brushes the pendant under the neckline of my sweater, hooking it out with a finger. "You never told me how you got this back."

I step away, forcing a smile. "I guess it was meant to be."

There's a heavy look in his eyes.

"Everything our parents did, it doesn't have to determine where we go, who we are." He reaches for my arm and pulls me toward the side of the house just out of sight.

Normally I'd brush him off but today feels like a day for truth.

"Adam, when we were together you didn't see me. You didn't try. You took for granted the time we spent together. And I'll take some of the blame, I should have asked for what I wanted."

"Which was what?"

"Connection. Compassion." I lift a shoulder. "You to go down on me once in a while."

He straightens up, an incredulous laugh on his lips. "You wished I'd gone down on you? That's why we broke up?"

"We broke up because you cheated," I correct. "That you never went down on me was just one more reason I came to accept it."

He steps closer. "I know you, Liv. Let's bail on this place and I can show you. You can tell me what you like and I'll give it to you."

I back toward the edge of the house, and swear I feel Sawyer's eyes on my back.

"You were my first everything, and I don't regret it. But it wasn't meant to be that way for either of us."

"I always figured it'd be you and me when everything shook down. I still do."

He bends closer, his lips brushing across mine before I can stop him.

He tastes like mint and nostalgia, and I press a hand to his chest to push him away.

A throat clearing behind us makes us turn.

Sawyer looms overhead, a glowering god ready to deal out punishment.

I rub the corner of my mouth, afraid he can see Adam on me.

"You're missing the party." His voice is dark and too quiet.

Adam smirks. "Just the opposite, Professor. We were saying how great it is."

Sawyer's going to kill Adam. He'll rip him in half and hide the body parts in the garden.

Scratch that. The way he looks, he's not going to bother hiding the body.

"We're fine, Professor Redmond," I insist, loading every word with meaning. "But thanks for your concern."

The intensity of his gaze pins me in place and it takes everything in me to break it.

I nod to Adam. "Come on, do you want to sign the poster?"

I return to the draped table, catching Sawyer's

eye for the briefest moment and willing him to relax. "They're going to blow it up and hang it in the…" I trail off as I realize the Sharpies aren't here.

I head inside to find them.

Nothing in the kitchen, so I head for the living room and spot a cup of pens there.

"Nice markers. Surprised Dr. Lancaster has a stash of them."

Adam's voice makes me jump as I lift the cup, which includes a few of my pink gel pens.

Before he can say anything more, a chest-high tornado tears into the room.

"Can I see the fish?" Andy demands when he stops in front of me.

"Sure, Andy. He's in my dance class," I explain as I lead the way.

"Shit, that's a big tank," Adam comments.

"It's no ocean but it holds a lot. Close as you can get to a habitat they're comfortable in."

"Tell me what they all are?" Andy asks.

I point them all out, and describe each of them. The catfish, the blue acara, the silver dollar fish.

"The black ghost knife fish is the coolest." I crouch around the side of the tank, pointing behind some seaweed, and Andy follows. "He comes from South America, and he's actually electric. Not enough to light you up, but it helps him find food."

"Can't he see it?"

"In here he can. But in the wild, not so much. He's nocturnal which is why he's hanging out back here."

"He's huge," Madison says, coming up behind us.

"About a foot, but they can grow to a foot and a half," I confirm. "And he has almost no true fins. Just pectoral ones."

"Are there more of them?"

"Not in here. They're a bit hard to handle and can get aggressive if they don't have their own space."

Come to think of it, it's no wonder Sawyer likes this fish. They have at least one thing in common.

The front door rings and I head for it.

When I pull the door wide, my smile freezes.

The man standing on the new porch is the last one I expect.

"Dean." He's here with his wife. "I didn't realize... Everyone's around the back."

He walks through the house and I shadow him, getting bad vibes the whole way. I hold the door for him and his wife to descend into the yard.

Sawyer glances up, his expression darkening as he takes in his new guests.

The dean clears his throat. "About the justification next week." My stomach tightens. "I wish you all the best."

"Thank you," I say, and mean it.

After the pressure of the last few weeks, it feels good to have the support of the department.

In the kitchen, I start cleaning things up. It's only a moment before I feel his presence at my back.

"You can't hide from me."

The hairs on my neck lift at his low voice. "Figured I'd help out in here since you were busy being a good host."

"So grabbing the kid and making a run for it wasn't an effort to escape?"

"I didn't want you going down for murder. I'm getting used to your bossy ass."

When I turn to face him, he's leaning against the wall, arms folded.

"Thought you knew what *exclusive* meant."

"He kissed me. He caught me by surprise, and if you believe it was anything more on my side than that, then you're a moron."

His eyes widen, as if he's surprised at the reprimand.

I want to go to him but I remember what he saw outside earlier, the look on his face.

"You did a great thing today."

"It's a BBQ, not Nobel Prize-winning research."

"The little moments matter. Without them, the big moments can't happen."

He crosses the kitchen, pinning me against the sink with his hips. "I kept telling myself I had no business being with you—that you were too young and on a different path. I thought I could teach you how to live without rules, but you taught me more."

He bends closer, near enough our mouths brush.

"I can't do this anymore, Olivia," he murmurs against my lips.

The words barely register.

He's so close and after hours of staring at him across the yard, watching him try to do right by the department and the team, it's all I can do not to wrap my legs around him and show him how damned proud I am.

"Do what?"

"No feelings. I told myself I'd try for you, because that's the one concession you asked of me. But I'm over trying to get through the day without thinking of you. Your smile. Your mind. Your fucking kindness. I've had a lot of dark times in my life, but if they brought me to you, I'm willing to square with them."

I pull back to stare in his dark, stormy eyes.

What I find makes my chest expand until I can't breathe.

Hope.

Trust.

Possibility.

"In the good moments and the bad ones," he goes on, "you're the first person I think of. You're in my bed and in my heart. And I'm not letting you out of either."

"No fucking way."

We both turn to see Adam standing in the door-way, phone in his hand.

23

OLIVIA

"Adam—"

He knows. It's plain in the horror on his face, the grim line of his mouth.

He turns and stalks back down the hall.

I run after him. "It's not what you think." He grunts in pain as I grab his bad arm, forcing him around.

His face is incredulous as he holds the phone up. "This isn't what I think?"

There's a picture of me and Sawyer, lips locked, my hands in his hair and his gripping my ass.

"What the hell, Liv? This is why you've been distant? I know you were under pressure from your parents, but you don't need him to get a good grade—"

"This is none of your business, Adam." Sawyer's

voice from behind me is the last thing I need. "You can't expect a woman to wait around for you."

Sawyer, don't.

"She's been my girlfriend since we were sixteen," Adam retorts, jaw jutting. "If you tried touching her then, you'd be in jail right now, asshole."

"If you try touching her now, you will be."

They're the same height. Sawyer always seemed bigger, because everything he is, he backs up.

"If you knew how to treat her, she wouldn't be with me. But you couldn't see what was right in front of you."

"Wow. This went back to the start of the school year?" Adam lurches toward me.

"It doesn't have to do with class, or the project."

"Really, Liv?" He gets close to me now, staring in my eyes. "So what, you get off on being his toy?"

"I'm not his toy."

I'm in love with him.

"Tell me this asshole pressured you."

He's like my parents, thinking I need protection.

I could make that look of horror and disgust on his face disappear. Say that it was all a mistake, save my own ass, and maybe convince him not to turn Sawyer in, too.

"What'd he do to you, babe?"

But it's not the truth. And right now, staring down

years of expectations in Adam's bright blue eyes, I'm not willing to bend.

I lift my chin. "He makes me come so hard I think I'm going to die."

Adam's eyes flash and he whirls on his heel for the back door, phone in hand.

SAWYER

When I descend the stairs, everyone knows something's wrong. It's plain on the stunned faces.

In the crowd, a few jump out at me. Madison looks morbidly fascinated. Royce is confused. Betty stands in one corner, her painted lips a round "o" of dismay. Daniel's shoulders slump, as if he was hoping we might get through this despite knowing deep down we couldn't.

Adam's standing next to the dean, eyes narrowed at me in accusation and betrayal. As if the fact that I dared touch Olivia is violating some greater evil than making his ex-girlfriend happier than she ever was with him.

But it's the dean who speaks first.

"Professor Redmond." He says the words as if he's shocked and appalled, but the way he steps forward says he's been waiting for this day. "A student has come to me with some intensely disturbing allegations. Allegations I'm inclined to believe because he's furnished evidence. We'll meet tomorrow afternoon to investigate once I've convened the disciplinary committee." Disciplinary sounds like firing squad. "In the meantime, we'll have your TA cover your classes, and the team's participation in the Stars competition will have to be put on hold."

No.

My students' expressions go from confused to horrified.

"What's going on?" Royce demands.

"Party's over." Daniel gestures toward the gate, willing people to leave.

My gaze locks with Olivia's.

"Miss Barclay," the dean goes on, "I strongly suggest you keep to yourself for the next little while. If you need counseling resources, student services can provide them. Please monitor your email, as the disciplinary committee will no doubt want to hear from you."

I can't talk to her now. Her eyes say she wants to, but that's going to make things worse.

Right after I told her I want more. She didn't have time to react.

Now, she goes with everyone else.

The strangest part was today had started to feel good. Like before the dean showed up, I didn't hate having everyone here.

The last time I was at this school, in this house, I felt like a missing piece from a different puzzle.

This afternoon, I was part of something. I never asked for this, and now that it's gone, my gut feels strangely empty.

24

SAWYER

The next day, everything moves in slow motion.

I get up, make coffee, shower, and pull on fresh clothes. As if it's any other day, except it's not.

I go in and meet with the half dozen men and two women on the disciplinary committee. The dean is, of course, chairing. At least there's one friendly face —Betty's at the end of the table, recording while also taking notes on her notebook computer. When her gaze meets mine, there's sympathy, not reproach.

As the hearing begins, phrases like gross misconduct, formal inquiry, probationary period drift through my brain.

The bottom line is they're investigating and I'll face professional sanctions. Possibly be fired.

"This is a despicable violation of school policy.

Do you deny having a relationship with your student?"

"I don't. But I wouldn't expect you to understand it, either."

The dean nearly drops his pen.

"When Miss Barclay and I met, it was outside of campus and school events. Our relationship began prior to her becoming my student."

That does catch him off guard. "In what capacity did you know her?"

"In the capacity that we met and had a connection," I toss back, even though he can't possibly understand. "Have you ever met another person and felt like they could see under your skin? And maybe it was because they were different, like they were meant to see you. Or hell, they simply took the time and checked their preconceptions at the door."

"So you had a physical connection. A sexual relationship would be gravely disturbing."

"More than an emotional one?"

"We're not here to debate—"

"You're the ones who spend all day theorizing." I pause. "I'm not here to explain our relationship to you. I'm telling you it didn't get in the way of me doing my job."

"Professor Redmond," a woman, the vice provost, begins, "our aim is not interfering with the personal lives of students and faculty. However, it is our responsibility to ensure there are no conflicts of interest, undue pressure, or unfair favoritism."

"And there was none."

"You agreed to supervise the Stars team and, I understand, appointed Miss Barclay the lead."

"If you'd seen what she did, you would've made her team lead, too." At their silence, I force myself to go on. "You want to know what kind of favoritism I gave her? The kind where I pushed her. Asked her to do more than she knew she could. Built up her confidence. I reminded her that when she gets out of bed and puts her feet on the floor in the morning, she has everything within herself to achieve her dreams. If that's not what faculty are expected to do, then forgive me, but I have no fucking clue what your job is."

They make some notes on their papers.

"My Stars team," I grind out. "I need assurances their work will resume."

"In light of these allegations and to protect the university, I can see no other recourse than to shut down our participation in the committee immediately," the dean says.

"What about that alumni donation we received?" Betty looks up from her computer, and I frown.

"What donation?"

Every set of eyes flies to the dean, who shifts in his seat. "Olivia Barclay's father made a contribution to the school."

"He requested the funds be directed to offset costs associated with the Stars project," Betty presses.

"And you responded by trying to compromise their efforts?" I say, my voice deadly low.

The only explanation is that he intended to use those funds for other purposes than the ones for which they were intended. It would make sense—if the team didn't make it past the next stage, he could tell the donor the funds were already used.

Except...Olivia's father is in financial difficulty. How could he support the team when he won't even help with tuition?

One of the women leans in. "Didn't the team qualify for nationals for the first time in a decade?"

I nod. "They're presenting a justification next week."

The vice provost purses her lips. "Dean, perhaps it makes sense to see how this next step of the process goes before making any decision about the team's future."

He realizes he's in a bind. He wants to shut the team down, either to screw me over or save money, and I wish I knew why.

For today, he can't.

That doesn't mean he won't try again tomorrow.

When he walks me to the door, it's my turn to pause. "How much did her father give?"

He hesitates. "Fifty thousand."

Fifty thousand. That number scratches at the back of my mind.

I'm two steps out the door when I reach for my phone.

25

OLIVIA

I get Sawyer's text in the middle of my final class of the day.

Repentant Asshole: The team can continue its work. I'm on probation pending the committee's investigation.

Liv: I need to see you.

Repentant Asshole: I'm going to New York to see Tate. We'll talk when I'm back.

.   .   .

My gut twists. I hadn't even thought about the implications for Sawyer's future business.

We haven't had a moment to talk since the party. I want to tell him I'm thinking of him every second. I hope he knows my mind's on him whether I'm at school, grabbing a dinner I can barely eat, or teaching.

When I wrap up my final class, I head to the library to meet with the team. Our justification is due in another week, and none of the drama on our campus is going to change that.

"This is where Madison talks about how we designed the tail functionality, mimicking nature. Then there's the section on the novel applications of circuitry...where is that section?"

I look up across the scattered photographs and printed pages at Royce, who's seated across the table in the campus library.

He shrugs, irritated. "I dunno where the section went. Adam was going to write it."

I turn to Adam, who's fiddling with the strap on his backpack. "I didn't see it, did you send it to me?"

He doesn't answer. Evidently he's still not speaking to me.

"Maybe you didn't see it because Professor Redmond didn't send it. It was crowded out of your inbox by all the dick pics."

I told Sawyer I would keep the team on track. I'm not the one on trial, which means my job should be easy.

In the past forty-eight hours, I scoped out the tank we'd use to demo our robot after the holidays.

Yet somehow, the team is falling apart.

We won't, I vow. If it's the only thing I can do, I'll hold this group together. We've worked too hard for this.

"This goal is bigger than all of us. Let's come together and make the justification happen." I think of Sawyer talking about how to pitch. "This is our chance to show the judges we're contenders."

"Don't blame Professor Redmond," I say.

"I don't. I blame you." Everyone in the study desks looks up at Adam's loud voice.

I've been leading this project and was thrilled by the chance to challenge myself and try new things. But at this moment, I'm flushed and overwhelmed.

Royce weighs in. "I get that she was your girlfriend but if it's about more than getting dick punched in the ego, then act like it."

"Thanks for having my back," I say, following Royce to the water fountain to refill my water bottle.

"What was your plan here?" he asks, turning.

"What do you mean?"

"There are only two ways out, no matter how

charmed your life is or what family you come from. Either you're the victim, the chick with wide eyes who got taken advantage of, or you're the girl who slept with her professor to get ahead."

"I'm not either of those."

He shrugs. "You think you're the first student to hook up with their professor? This is an age-old story. And there's no other way this story ends."

"Okay, everybody. That's all for tonight." The smile is harder to summon than usual as I shepherd my guppies toward the door.

"...picking up?" A familiar male voice enters my consciousness.

"Yeah, I'm picking up. Are you?" An even more familiar female voice has me looking up.

Kat's dressed in a loose blazer and skirt, arms folded as she leans against the wall.

Next to her is Daniel.

"Ah, this one must be yours," Kat says as Andy trots over to his dad, showing off some badass chassés.

"He's the only boy," says one of the girls solemnly.

Kat eyes up Andy. "So basically, you're going to be a star."

He giggles, but Daniel's attention, his curiosity and appreciation, is locked on my friend.

"Which one's yours?"

"That one." She points at me and I cross to them, laughing.

"Daniel, this is my roommate Kat."

"Roommate. As in…"

"At Russell. Yeah."

I bite my cheek while I watch him process.

Kat, oblivious, grabs my arm. "Come on, get your ass changed. Jules and I are kidnapping you."

"For what?" I demand, but she won't say.

Five minutes later, we're on the bus. "What's with the hot mom's PTA meeting getup?" I ask.

She pops a hip before she drops into a seat. "We had oral presentations today. I want to be a therapist, so I'm sure going to dress the part."

"But you want to be a sex therapist."

"Oh in that case, let me get my fishnets."

She pulls me off at a bus stop and I trail her to our usual pub. It's more than half full despite it being barely dinnertime.

"Hoes Over Brews: All Hoes, No Bros edition."

Jules is waiting with a table and a gift bag.

"What's this for?" I ask.

"To remind you how awesome you are. That we see you and we love you. You always look out for other people and now, we're looking out for you."

I reach for the pink tissue paper, tugging it out.

Inside the bag, my fingers land on soft fabric.

Lingerie? I pull it out, holding it up...

"It's a sash," Kat says. "The kind beauty queens have."

"But it says #1 Roommate."

"Zero propaganda. You've always been there for us. We want you to know we're here for you, no matter what," Jules says. "Now put it on."

I drape the satin over my head, feeling like the biggest nerd ever.

I'll also fight anyone in this bar who tries to take it from me.

This is what college is supposed to be about. People with different experiences coming together and learning from each other.

"Thank you," I say and mean it.

"I know it's been a rough semester, but we got you," Kat emphasizes. "All we have to do is get through exams, then we have two whole weeks off on the other side."

She's right.

"Hey, what's that?" I nod to a slip of paper sticking out of Jules' bag.

"It's a script for a new drama society production. Auditions are next week."

It helps to catch up with them, to hear Jules talk about the play, and Kat laugh over experiments.

"I need you both to participate in my project as experimental subjects when we get back from the holidays."

"You can't cut into my brain," Jules says evenly.

Kat grins. "All you have to do is show up at the lab for an hour. You get twenty bucks for your time. What do you say, Liv?"

I shift in my seat, slinging an arm over the back of my chair. "What are you testing?"

"Come on, friendship is thicker than blood."

"I'm not sure that's the saying. But okay." My lips twitch.

I'm holding the team together by my fingernails. Sawyer's in big trouble. But in another week, I'll do the justification and have exams, then we all have winter break. Time for everyone to decompress.

I have to hang on until then.

Plus Sawyer and I haven't had a chance to talk since his confession at the party.

I'm over trying to get through the day without thinking of you.

My heart feels like it's going through a blender since he left.

By the time we leave the bar three hours later, I might not be feeling relaxed, but I'm resolved. I know I'll figure this out, and my friends have my back.

We take the bus to campus, and I look up at the stars as we cross campus to our apartment.

When we head up the stairs and Kat fumbles for her keys for the door at home, my phone vibrates again.

But this time, it's not Sawyer.

"What the hell..." I pull up.

"What is it?" Jules asks, padding over to me.

"An email from the Stars committee. Confirmation of our presentation tomorrow..." I trail off. "This must be a joke."

"Ifrtwsnxtwik?" Kat says through a mouthful of toothpaste. She rolls her eyes and spits it out in the sink, returning a moment later. "I thought it was next week?"

"It is." I read the email again, frantic.

There's no reason they would've moved it. Except...

The department contact copied on the email isn't Sawyer.

"Son of a bitch."

26

OLIVIA

"Livvy honey?" Betty pulls up to the bench outside the dean's office where I've been camped out since seven this morning, a bag and coffee in one hand and keys in the other. "What's wrong?"

"I need to see the dean. I emailed him last night, but he didn't respond."

When he arrives half an hour later, I jump up off the bench. "There's been a mistake. The Stars competition changed the date for our presentation to today."

"Oh yes. I reached out to them and requested the change in timeline. Professor Redmond didn't want the investigation to interfere with your work, and I'm inclined to agree."

"But Professor Redmond isn't here," I emphasize. "We have no supervisor."

"I'm taking over those duties until further notice."

When I pictured presenting the justification, I was nervous. This is a big deal to our team, and sets the stage for whether we're going to have a shot at actually winning.

But I always imagined it with Sawyer at my side.

Not only is he gone, but the man in his place wants us to fail.

The dean checks his watch. "I look forward to seeing you in the presentation immediately after lunch. If you need anything in the interim, don't hesitate to let me know."

The smile he pastes on makes me wretch.

I pull out my phone, fingers smashing against the keyboard.

Liv: We have an EMERGENCY. Meet me at the lab now. Skip class. I don't care what it takes, just get there.

"You're joking. This is a joke. Or a bad fucking dream," Royce says flatly when I get to the lab.

"I wish." I pace the room, tugging on the hair I didn't have time to curl this morning. "We have to do the presentation at one this afternoon."

"We can't," Adam replies.

"We have to pull together," I tell Adam. "You might not like Sawyer much right now"—he flinches at the familiarity—"but he helped set us up to do this right. If we can just pull together on this, I'll do whatever you guys want after next week."

"But we're not ready," Madison points out. "And we don't have any visuals."

The presentation was supposed to include a demo of the bot.

I need Sawyer. He's the one who got us into this. He could get us out.

I dial his number, each ring making my stomach flip.

Come on, come on, come on.

No answer.

I force my brain to function, feel the synapses firing as I pace the room.

The photos on the walls aren't of machinery but of the moon landing, a smiling child in a hospital.

That's when it clicks.

"We don't need the robot. This is about what's

possible, right? We can talk to them about our vision." I pull out my phone and dial my roommates. "Jules, Kat, I need you guys."

We go to Lancaster's with a truck, and I use the key under the back door mat to get us in.

"We need to be fast," I emphasize. "The tank has a backup power supply, but the fish can't go without the pump to circulate the water for long."

We have to take the tank off the power supply for the drive over, and I'm counting the minutes until we can get it hooked back up on campus.

If these fish die, I can't handle it.

I don't breathe until the pump starts up when we plug it in at the design lab, sending bubbles that rise to the surface. The black ghost knife fish peeks out from between seaweed near the back of the tank.

My fingers itch to dial Sawyer's number, but Madison interrupts my thoughts.

"We have to do this. Now."

The presentation is set up in the lab with Betty's help, three judges' video feeds spread across the huge screen pulled down from the ceiling.

The dean watches on from the corner, arms folded. I go over our presentation in my mind.

I squeeze my necklace in my fist before launching into my comments.

"Most engineering is about conquering the world

around us. From the advent of the wheel, and fire, and tools used for hunting right up to the microchip, we've tried to become better than nature. It's the easier way—it's profitable, even if we don't question it.

"But we can't stop death, we can't lift everyone out of poverty. We're still human," I emphasize. "So what do we miss while we're trying to conquer the world? We miss the chance to understand it. To exist as part of it, alongside it."

I step to the side of the tank.

"Oceans cover seventy percent of the earth's surface. They're full of life, more species than on land, and the most incredible diversity. Take fish. There's research showing they have memories. That they're social. They even recognize music. If we don't learn about the world around us, we're going to change it profoundly and lose all that information forever.

"I understand that most of the projects are about commercially viable technologies. But technology isn't about conquering, it's about learning. Working with the systems around us, not crushing them. That's what we want to build. A robot that helps these ecosystems, not hurts them."

We finish our presentation and the judges grill us.

It's not perfect, but I feel alive and free.

After, I cut a look toward the door as if expecting to see Sawyer there because I can't remember feeling that way without him.

But he's not there.

"You crushed it," Kat informs me, wrapping an arm around my neck as I trip up the walk to the Omega house that night.

"I wouldn't go that far."

"She did," Madison says, coming up next to us. "They can't possibly turn us down after that."

"So what happens now?"

"We get feedback from the judges. If they approve it, we get extra funding to help with building our project."

"Which we'll need for the tank," I add. "And to make the robot float."

We head inside, the party already in full swing.

"What is it?" I prod Madison as she grimaces.

"The last time we were here, I played that video."

"Yeah, that was pretty shitty."

She sighs. "You fucked our professor. We're even."

I make my way toward the kitchen, where frat

brothers are pouring from a keg into cups. "Except I never wanted to hurt anyone or screw anything up. You were trying to do exactly that."

I take a cup and pass it to her.

"It wasn't my idea," she says as she takes it.

A second cup is pressed into my hand, but my attention is on Madison. "Whose was it?"

She looks over the room where Adam's with a group of guys.

I freeze, cup bending in my grip. "No."

"How do you think I got the video? One of his friends took it."

He wanted to break me down, to make me weak and vulnerable.

What I'm doing with Sawyer was wrong, but this kind of backstabbing is acceptable?

I weave through the crowd to my ex and grab his phone out of his pocket.

"Hey. What are you doing?"

The passcode is the same one he's always had—the day, month, and year the Knicks last won the NBA championship, and well before either of us was born.

Scrolling through his photos, there are a lot that turn my stomach. But I find the video I'm looking for, dated the night from Velvet.

"You took this video." My voice shakes with accusation.

"It's not like that. One of the guys did."

"And he sent it to you. And you gave it to Madison to post."

His jaw flexes. "Liv, come on. I thought if people gave you a hard time, it might make you realize it was better when we were together."

"It was better when I was with someone who lied to me and cheated on me?" He lunges for the phone, still hampered by the sling, and I hold the device away. "You're unbelievable. I can't believe I felt badly for you."

I shove through the crowd toward the door.

I always appreciated that Adam understood our families and the pressures to fit in, and admired how the scheming and manipulation seemed to roll right off him.

But evidently he was taking notes the whole time.

When I'm making my way out to the porch, my phone jumps in my pocket.

The name on the call display has my heart leaping. "Hi," I answer, breathless, as I crane my neck to make sure Adam's not behind me. "Where are you?"

"On my way back into town."

His voice is so familiar, I ache.

There's unresolved stuff between us, but I want to

see him, want to crawl into his arms and feel his hair tickle my forehead when he leans over me.

"I need to see you." His words have the knot in my chest loosening, a breath whooshing out.

I look around the frat party. "I'm outside the Omega house. We are—were," I amend, "celebrating. I can be at your place in half an hour."

He hangs up and I'm left standing, my jaw on the concrete walkway.

I glance across the road and do a double take.

His car is there.

"What the hell are you doing?" Adam demands, appearing out of nowhere.

I spin to face him. "You were right. There are some mistakes you can't take back. And there are others I'd make again, exactly the same way."

I toss his phone at him. He lunges for it, twisting and falling onto his injured arm.

I don't stick around.

Sawyer buzzes the driver's window down and I sprint across the street to meet him. His hair is wild around his face, and there are dark circles under his eyes. His firm mouth is pursed but his eyes leap when they lock with mine, his hands gripping the steering wheel.

"Get in."

Adrenaline surges through me and I round the

hood, one last look over my shoulder at the party. A dozen people are standing on the lawn staring and pointing. Adam is slack-jawed on the ground.

"Hope your day was better than mine," Sawyer says as I shift inside.

I lower my window, adjusting the passenger side mirror. "Everyone accused me of sleeping with my professor to get ahead."

"And did you?"

I reach for lip gloss in my bag, slick it on, then recap the gloss and tuck it away. "Not to get ahead."

"Then why?"

He accelerates down the street, the Mercedes tearing down the road in a combination of power and elegance.

"Because every second I'm not with him, life's not as good as it could be."

Sawyer exhales heavily and I glance over at his profile. If there's a more beautiful man in the world, I've never met him. I'm getting high on his scent and our proximity.

But his next words halt all thoughts of making up with him.

"You gave the fifty-thousand dollars from my father to Russell's engineering department."

I play with the strap on my bag, my stomach tightening. "Surprise...?"

"It was impulsive and doing it behind my back was duplicitous."

"I can't tell which one you're mad about."

"Both," he grits out.

"It was me making a decision for myself. I wasn't about to lose this project," I go on as familiar neighborhoods pass.

When we get to his place, my attention is captured by the SOLD sign on the lawn. "What's with the sign?"

"Accepted an offer this morning."

Wow.

"Where will you live when you come back after the winter break…" I trail off, because I'm an idiot.

Of all the times I wanted to be mature, to make my own decisions and think about my future, I never understood what that meant. Not really.

But he does.

"You're not coming back."

His dark eyes search mine. "No."

My stomach falls through my feet, the earth tilting.

I want to be sick. Or to scream. Or to rewind until the second before I saw that awful sign, when the world was crashing down but we still had each other.

I'm out the door before he can grab me.

"Olivia…"

I head up the walk to the steps, not sure where I'm going, but standing still is impossible.

My knees give out and I sink to the sturdy porch, the one Sawyer built with his bare hands this fall.

He silently sits next to me and pulls me into his arms.

"When do you leave?"

"Next week."

Tears burn the backs of my eyes.

I hate that I can't think about existing without him. I hate that he made me into a person who wants more out of life, and now he's walking away and I don't know where to find that.

He lifts my chin, cupping my face in his large hands and forcing my watery gaze to his. "Come to New York with me."

Disbelief slams into me. I search his face, because there's no way he said that. "Are you serious?"

"Transfer schools. You have good grades, we can get you into NYU. Hell, maybe even Columbia. None of this will follow you."

My lungs expand until I think I might burst. Like a dream, the future paints itself behind my eyes. "You're actually crazy."

"We'll start over. We can get a place in the city. Bring Captain Jack and every one of those damned fish. We'll find somewhere for you to dance. Tell me you want to."

"I want to," I whisper. "More than anything."

"Good. Because I don't want to wake up without you."

He drags me into his lap and traps my mouth with his.

He's heat and fire and the acceptance and admiration I've craved my entire life.

I thought once I experienced those feelings, my desire would fade.

Instead, it gets stronger.

I want to be wanted.

I need to be needed.

Not some perfect version of myself, but this real, raw one.

But I'd be leaving my friends.

My school.

The Stars competition...

I lock the thoughts away and kiss him back.

27

SAWYER

"We're gonna miss you around here," says Daniel as I finish packing up my father's things in boxes for Goodwill.

A few items are tagged in separate piles to be sent to his academic colleagues.

"You'll get over it. People leave."

"Doesn't mean it doesn't suck." Daniel claps me on the back. "Stay in touch, yeah? Or I'll come to the city and hunt your ass down."

There's a knock on the door, and he pushes it wide to reveal Betty.

"I thought you might like something of him to remember." I step back and gesture to a pile of items on the hall table next to the bowl of apples. "These were from his office. Favorite books. Cufflinks. I don't know what would make you think of him."

She beams. "That's sweet of you. I don't need things to remember. He's in my heart."

I turn that over as I cross to the fish tank.

The team borrowed it for their demo, and it's not centered back on the table. I kneel down and adjust it, finding a piece of tape on the bottom.

For Olivia Barclay.

"He wanted her to have them," I murmur.

"What's that?"

I shake my head.

Captain Jack lurks near the back in his favorite patch of seaweed. Bright clownfish dot the clear water.

It's going to be a pain in the ass to ship to New York, but we'll figure it out. I'm sure as hell bringing it because it makes Olivia smile.

And she makes me smile.

I still can't believe she's coming with me. Russell U might be cutting me loose, but I don't need them.

A shape on top of the water, a few inches length, grabs my attention.

A single blue fish.

Belly up.

My stomach turns. It must have happened after the students took the tank to campus for their presentation.

"Your father made mistakes," Betty ventures, not noticing. "Especially where you were concerned."

I force my focus back to her. "I don't know why he took me in. We clashed at every turn."

"Surely it wasn't that bad."

"The night I left, he accused me of ruining the dean's career. Said I'd never make anything of myself. I was afraid he might be right."

Betty sighs. "He made a mistake, Sawyer. Every time you set a toe out of line, he swore it was his fault. He watched you go out in the world and make your own way, and he realized he was wrong. You weren't breaking the rules, you were creating something beautiful," she goes on. "But in order for them to be their best, we have to go through the hard times."

Maybe there's something to it.

Darkness begets light.

Ugliness reveals beauty.

Cruelty shows us the gift of kindness.

"There's a file drawer upstairs I haven't been able to get into. Do you have any idea what the combination might be? I've tried his birthday, the date he got tenure, the address, everything I can think of."

She screws up her face. "Try this." She writes down a series of six numbers on a slip of paper. "I'll see you at the disciplinary committee meeting in a few hours."

My abs tighten as I see her out.

I memorize the number—it's meaningless to me—as I scoop the fish out of the tank and flush it.

Then I take the stairs up to my father's office and go to the file cabinet, trying the password Betty suggested.

It works.

Unlike the rest of his office that was bursting with papers and electronics, this contains only a few slim files.

The first is from the adoption agency.

The letter on top is from him, addressed to them.

...hasty decision...

...entirely unsuitable...

...no possible successful outcome...

I set the letter down, numb.

He tried to send me back. After he took me in, he didn't only berate me and ignore me. The man who put a roof over my head wanted me gone.

Just like everyone else in my life.

Cherry: Can we meet up?

· · ·

Sawyer: I have a few minutes before I'm due to see the disciplinary committee.

I step off the elevator to see her already waiting in the hallway in dark jeans and black boots, her hair spilling over the shoulders of her jacket.

My heart kicks at her presence. She's not a student. She's a woman, and a dream, and every chance of a life I never let myself believe I could have.

And she's mine.

"Hey."

"Hi."

She lets me drag her against me, her lips soft welcoming under mine.

The letter messed with my head, but she can fix it. I believe in the power she has.

"I have something to show you." She pulls up her phone and holds it out. "Our justification feedback."

Dear Russell U team, we were impressed with your commitment to design and ecology. We are awarding you a twenty-thousand-dollar stipend and inviting you to continue to the next round.

Her laugh is incredulous. "Can you believe it?"

Olivia presses up on her toes to throw her arms around my neck.

She's thrilled the same way I am to see her, but it's not my presence that's got her on a high.

It's the email.

A ribbon of ice snakes through me—a warning I want to ignore but can't.

I pull back a second before she can.

"You're not coming to New York."

Her face falls, and my answer is plain on her face before she forms the words. "I can't."

It's a spear in my gut. The end of the dreams I let myself dream these past weeks, ones I never should have allowed in the first place.

"Because of Adam? Madison? Royce? This school? What do you owe it? They turned on you the moment they found out about us."

Her dark brows pull together.

"I want to stick this out. You taught me not to lean on anyone, to stand on my own. Are you saying I shouldn't?"

Fuck.

She's not wrong, but the letter from my father rises to the front of my mind.

...hasty decision...

...entirely unsuitable...

...no possible successful outcome...

She has her whole future ahead of her, and I'm not that.

"Sawyer, don't look at me like that. Please," she whispers. "This doesn't have to be the end—"

"It's not the end." Her brows lift but I press on. "Because there was no beginning. I wanted you because I couldn't have you. It wouldn't have worked beyond these walls."

She recoils in shock. "You don't mean that."

"I do. You helped me realize it. I got caught up in the same thing I was selling you. Freedom, at another's hands. Anarchy. At some point, I forgot those things aren't stable."

"Don't say it," she whispers, emotion choking her voice. She reaches for me and I wave her hand away.

If she touches me, I'll implode.

I wanted her to be free to express herself, and that's what she's doing—but not to her family, her piece of shit ex, she's doing it to me. Telling me what she wants, I can't give her.

It hurts so fucking badly.

Worse than my mom leaving.

Worse than my dad watching me walk out the door.

Worse than my own partner believe a lying girl over me.

Because I can see in her eyes that she cares. She wants me.

But it's not enough.

She wants this more.

My gaze drags over her from her toes to her lips. "You're beautiful. Ripe. Addictive. Once I had a taste, I wanted more. I'm not a man who denies himself. But even the most ravenous animal is eventually sated."

Her eyes cool on mine, as if she's looking into me, through me. "You're not an animal. You're a man. But not even an animal can get enough of what it doesn't truly need."

"Meaning?"

"You crave love, but you can't name it and you can't ask for it, and when it knocks on your door you turn it away because you're terrified once you let it in, it could slip out in the night."

Her words sink into my skin, my soul.

I'm losing her.

No.

No, I won't.

This time, I'll—

"Professor Redmond." The door opens and Betty looks out. "They're ready for you."

I turn my back on Olivia and enter the room, shutting the door at my back.

"Dr. Redmond," the vice provost begins. "Thank you for accepting our invitation to attend this meeting."

"I figured it was more of a demand than an invitation."

Betty shoots me a look that says not to joke.

"We've come to a decision regarding your case, and..."

There's a noise outside.

One of the members goes to the door to tell whoever's outside to cut it out, but Royce steps inside, followed by Adam and Madison. Olivia trails them.

Royce turns to the faculty, holding up his phone. "We got through to the final round of the competition. That's never happened in Russell U history."

"You deserve it. But the celebration needs to move elsewhere." I nod to the table of startled academics.

Royce is the next one to look up at me. "You've helped us. Who are they going to stick us with if you're not here?"

"I've already spoken with another faculty member to cover the commitment. Dr. Greene."

"Dr. Greene is eighty," Adam blurts.

Madison nods. "We want you to stay. We won't let you leave."

"We were about to render our verdict," the woman says pointedly. "You all need to leave."

"If you want me to go, you can say it in front of my students."

She frowns. "Fine. Professor Redmond, the relationship you had with a student was ill-advised and unethical. But because the student is of age, there is nothing illegal. Further...we found no evidence that it unfairly affected your other students. In fact, the students in question wrote letters of support on your behalf."

My head snaps around to my students, then back to the administrators.

This isn't how I expect it to sound.

"We would like you to remain at Russell next semester."

I swear I've misheard.

There's no way they want me here.

"Thank fuck," Royce blurts. Madison gasps and even Adam looks relieved.

Olivia's eyes widen with hope and emotions that threaten to gut me.

There's a chance.

We can make this work.

I'm here and so is she. The woman who sees me at my best and my worst.

The second we're out of here, we'll set things right.

The vice provost rises from her seat. "Could

everyone but Professor Redmond and Miss Barclay please leave the room?"

Madison, Royce, and Adam head for the hall. Once the door closes behind them, the room is quiet.

The dean of engineering clears his throat. But it's not me he's looking at—it's Olivia.

"I spoke to your parents this morning. I wanted to keep them apprised of your situation, as a concerned parent and particularly given his support of the department. The thing is, he had no idea what I was talking about."

Olivia tenses at my side.

Hidden from view by our bodies, my fingers itch to thread through hers behind her back, but she's too far away.

"Olivia Barclay," the dean begins, "for your conduct, including possessing a copy of a faculty keycard and lying about an alumni donation, Russell University has decided you are no longer fit to attend this institution. You are hereby expelled."

Thank you for reading *Collide*! I hope you loved Sawyer and Olivia's story.

WHEN OLIVIA'S FUTURE IS TORN FROM HER
FINGERTIPS, CAN SHE AND SAWYER DEFY THE ODDS AND
FIGHT FOR THEIR FUTURE?
FIND OUT IN *CLAIM*.

If you enjoyed *Collide*, I'd be so grateful if you would leave a short review wherever you picked up this book.

Reviews are one of the best ways to help support indie authors (including me!), and to help readers find new books they'll love.

Thank you!

xoxo,

Piper

BOOKS BY PIPER LAWSON

KING OF THE COURT SERIES

After being dumped and losing my job the same week, the last thing my broken heart needs is a rebound.

A steamy, grumpy sunshine sports romance featuring a woman down on her luck, a star basketball player with a filthy mouth, and a connection neither of them can deny.

OFF-LIMITS SERIES

Turns out the beautiful man from the club is my new professor... But he wasn't when he kissed me.

Off-Limits is a forbidden age gap college romance series. Find out what happens when the beautiful man from the club is Olivia's hot new professor.

WICKED SERIES

Rockstars don't chase college students. But Jax Jamieson never followed the rules.

Wicked is a new adult rock star series full of nerdy girls, hot rock stars, pet skunks, and ensemble casts you'll want to be friends with forever.

RIVALS SERIES

At seventeen, I offered Tyler Adams my home, my life, my heart. He stole them all.

Rivals is an angsty new adult series. Fans of forbidden romance, enemies to lovers, friends to lovers, and rock star romance will love these books.

ENEMIES SERIES

I sold my soul to a man I hate. Now, he owns me.

Enemies is an enthralling, explosive romance about an American DJ and a British billionaire. If you like wealthy, royal alpha males, enemies to lovers, travel or sexy romance, this series is for you!

TRAVESTY SERIES

My best friend's brother grew up. Hot.

Travesty is a steamy romance series following best friends who start a fashion label from NYC to LA. It contains best friends brother, second chances, enemies to lovers, opposites attract and friends to lovers stories. If you like sexy, sassy romances, you'll love this series.

PLAY SERIES

I know what I want. It's not Max Donovan. To hell with his money, his gaming empire, and his joystick.

Play is an addictive series of standalone romances with slow burn tension, delicious banter, office romance and unforgettable characters. If you like smart, quirky, steamy enemies-to-lovers, contemporary romance, you'll love Play.

MODERN ROMANCE SERIES

When your rich, handsome best friend asks you to be his fake girlfriend? Say no.

Modern Romance is a smart, sexy series of contemporary romances following a set of female friends running a relationship marketing company in NYC. If you enjoy hot guys who treat their families like gold, fun antics, dirty talk, real characters, steamy scenes, badass heroines and smart banter, you'll love the Modern Romance series.

ABOUT THE AUTHOR

Piper Lawson is a WSJ and USA Today bestselling author of smart and steamy romance.

She writes women who follow their dreams, best friends who know your dirty secrets and love you anyway, and complex heroes you'll fall hard for.

Piper lives in Canada with her tall and brilliant husband. She's a sucker for dark eyes, dark coffee, and dark chocolate.

For a complete reading list, visit
www.piperlawsonbooks.com/books

Subscribe to Piper's VIP email list
www.piperlawsonbooks.com/subscribe

amazon.com/author/piperlawson

bookbub.com/authors/piper-lawson

instagram.com/piperlawsonbooks

facebook.com/piperlawsonbooks

goodreads.com/piperlawson

ACKNOWLEDGMENTS

Sawyer and Liv's story has taken me on a ride I never expected. I have loved every second of going deeper into their world.

How is it possible their highs and lows feel as if they transcend college firsts, but are also the perfect example of that time? No idea. But they're so real and visceral to me, and I wouldn't have it any other way.

Collide wouldn't have happened without the support of my awesome readers, including my ARC team. You ladies provide endless enthusiasm, cheerleading, and help spreading the word. I could NOT do it without you.

Thank you Tal, Suzanne, and Tina for your honest (and timely!) feedback. Becca, thank you for knowing the characters in my head better than I do. Erica, thank you for polishing, cheerleading and catching all the little things.

Thank you Regina for the perfect image. And Dani for your sage advice and for helping my stories find their way to readers who'll cherish them like I do.

And Annette Brignac and Michelle Clay... I don't know how I published a sentence before you. Don't ever leave me.

Thank you all from the bottom of my heart. The best part of author life is having YOU in it.

Love always,
Piper